"I'll return to my — Maggy said. Not — **you and why do you care if some barista in a photograph looks like an old, dead** ~~queen?~~

Reza drew himself up to his full height. He looked down at her with all the authority and consequence that had been pounded into every inch of him all his life, even when his own father had failed to live up to the crown he now wore himself.

"I am Leopoldo Maximillian Otto, King of the Constantines," he informed her. "But you may call me by my private family nickname, Reza."

She let out a sharp, hard sound that was not quite a laugh and thrust his mobile back at him. "I don't want to call you anything."

"That will be awkward, then."

Reza took possession of his mobile, studying the way she deliberately kept her fingers from so much as brushing his, as if he was poisonous. He was a king, not a snake. How this creature dared to treat him—*him*—with such disrespect baffled him, but did nothing to assuage that need that still worked inside him. She confounded him, and he didn't like it.

But that didn't change the facts. Much less what would be gained by presenting his people with the lost Santa Domini princess as his bride.

He met her gaze then. And held it. "Because one way or another, you are to be my wife."

Wedlocked!

Conveniently wedded, passionately bedded!

Whether there's a debt to be paid, a will
to be obeyed or a business to be saved...
she's got no choice but to say, "I do!"

But these billionaire bridegrooms have got another
think coming if they think marriage will be that easy...

Soon their convenient brides become
the object of an *inconvenient* desire!

Find out what happens after the vows in

The Billionaire's Defiant Acquisition
by Sharon Kendrick

One Night to Wedding Vows
by Kim Lawrence

Wedded, Bedded, Betrayed
by Michelle Smart

Expecting a Royal Scandal
by Caitlin Crews

Trapped by Vialli's Vows
by Chantelle Shaw

A Diamond for Del Rio's Housekeeper
by Susan Stephens

Baby of His Revenge
by Jennie Lucas

Bound by His Desert Diamond
by Andie Brock

Look out for more **Wedlocked!** stories
coming soon!

Caitlin Crews

BRIDE BY ROYAL DECREE

HARLEQUIN PRESENTS®

Recycling programs for this product may not exist in your area.

ISBN-13: 978-0-373-06041-2

Bride by Royal Decree

First North American publication 2017

Copyright © 2017 by Caitlin Crews

Printed in U.S.A.

www.Harlequin.com

USA TODAY bestselling and RITA® Award–nominated author **Caitlin Crews** loves writing romance. She teaches her favorite romance novels in creative-writing classes at places like UCLA Extension's prestigious Writers' Program, where she finally gets to utilize the MA and PhD in English literature she received from the University of York in England. She currently lives in California with her very own hero and too many pets. Visit her at caitlincrews.com.

Books by Caitlin Crews

Harlequin Presents

Castelli's Virgin Widow
At the Count's Bidding
Undone by the Sultan's Touch
Not Just the Boss's Plaything
A Devil in Disguise
In Defiance of Duty
The Replacement Wife
Princess from the Past

One Night With Consequences

The Guardian's Virgin Ward

The Billionaire's Legacy

The Return of the Di Sione Wife

Wedlocked!

Expecting a Royal Scandal

The Chatsfield

Greek's Last Redemption

Scandalous Sheikh Brides

Protecting the Desert Heir
Traded to the Desert Sheikh

Visit the Author Profile page at Harlequin.com for more titles.

To anyone, like me, who dreamed
they were really a princess...

CHAPTER ONE

THERE WERE FEW things Maggy Strafford liked less than scrubbing the coffee shop floor—or really any floor, for that matter. Dental surgery. The stomach flu. Any and all memories of her unfortunate childhood in foster care. Still, there she was on her hands and knees, dutifully attacking an unidentifiable sticky patch on the hardwood floors of The Coffee Queen in the tiny, tourist-rich hamlet of Deanville, Vermont, just down the road from one of the state's most famous resorts. Because it was her job as the most recently hired barista on this, the first night the owners had trusted her enough to close up shop.

And for once in the bumpy carnival ride that had been her life since she'd been found by the side of the road as a feral child with no memory of where she'd come from, Maggy was determined to keep her job. Even if it involved scrubbing unidentified sticky things off the floor of a coffee shop in almost the middle of nowhere, Vermont.

She scowled when the bell on the door rang, announcing the arrival of one more coffee-obsessed tourist who couldn't, apparently, read the closed sign she'd flipped over on the glass. Or spare a glance inside to see all the chairs flipped up on the tables, clearly indicating the shop was closed for business. Or notice Maggy herself, there on her hands and knees on the floor, obviously not manning the espresso machine.

"We're closed," she called out as a blast of chilly winter air rushed in, swirling around her and making her wish she hadn't stripped off her thick sweater to do the end of day wipe down. She did not say, *which you can see right there on the door, assuming you can read*, because that kind of knee-jerk, snotty response was the Old Maggy. New Maggy was kinder and gentler. And had thus been steadily and gainfully employed for the past five months.

With that in mind, she summoned a smile as she tossed her sponge back into her bucket with enough force to make the brown water slosh alarmingly. She hated smiling on command. She wasn't exactly made for customer service and never had been, as her spotty employment record attested. But New Maggy knew better than to share her real feelings with anyone, especially not the customers, and who cared how rich and correspondingly annoying they were. Her real and inevitably prickly feelings were her personal business and best kept hidden away if she wanted to keep her current, surprisingly okay, situation. Which she did. So she aimed all her teeth at the door when she looked up.

And her half-assed smile toppled straight off her face.

Two heavily muscled and stern-faced men in dark suits that strained over their physiques strode inside, muttering into earpieces in a language that was definitely not English. They paid Maggy no mind whatsoever as she gaped up at them, moving swiftly past her where she knelt on the floor with a certain brisk efficiency that made her stomach flip over. In warning and a little bit of panic. She knew she needed to jump up and deal with them somehow, which her ingrained fight-or-flight monitor suggested meant running the hell away rather than confronting either one of them.

She braced herself to do just that.

But then another man walked in, flanked by two more muscle-bound goons with earpieces and cold, grim eyes. And giant, ugly handguns on their hips. *Guns.* The obvious security detail peeled off, each one taking a position at one of the front windows, all dark suits, hard gazes, and grim, bulging arms.

The man in the center took another step or two inside the coffee shop and then simply stood there, gazing down at Maggy as if he'd anointed himself the new messiah.

Maggy was no particular fan of arrogant men. Or

men at all, if she was honest, given the less than stellar examples she'd encountered over the years, particularly in the foster care system. But she found her usual defense mechanisms—those being her smart mouth and her willingness to wield it first and ask questions later—seemed to have fled her completely.

Because the man standing there above her as if there was a sound track playing the "Hallelujah Chorus" as he did so was…something else.

He stood as if it was commonplace for him to find all sorts of people on their knees before him. As if, in fact, he was faintly bored that there was one more person at his feet. She should have loathed him on sight.

Instead, Maggy's heart slammed against her ribs—and didn't stop. She told herself he was nothing special. Just another man, and an evidently pompous one at that. Obviously, ridiculously, eye-rollingly wealthy like so many of the people who descended on this little après ski town in the winters. They were a dime a dozen here, leaping in and out of their gleaming four-wheel-drive monstrosities and blinding people with their lazy, too-white smiles. They draped themselves over all the best tables in the town's restaurants, jacked up the prices in all the village's boutiques with their willingness to purchase T-shirts for upwards of a hundred dollars, and cluttered up the coffee shops with their paragraph-long orders of joyless fake drinks.

This guy is nothing special at all, Maggy assured herself, still gazing up at him as if this was a church and she'd taken to her knees to do a few decades of a very specific sort of rich man rosary on a dark winter evening. *This guy is interchangeable with all the rest out there.*

But that was a lie.

He was extraordinary.

Something seemed to *hum* from him, some intense power or perhaps that sheer *certainty* that seemed stamped into his very bones. It was more than simple arrogance. It was more than the tanned faces, white teeth, and high-end vehicles idling by the curb that the others in this town assumed made them demigods. It made it hard to look away from him, as if he claimed all the light in the shop—in the town, in the whole of New England—for himself. And he wasn't exactly hard to look at, she was forced to concede. He wore dark trousers and boots that Maggy could tell at a glance cost more than the fancy SUVs the usual tony ski bums drove. He wore one of those expensively flattering winter coats that exuded upper-class elegance and deep masculinity at once. He was tall, and not just because she was still kneeling. He had wide shoulders and the kind of rangy, offhandedly athletic physique that suggested he spent a lot of very hard, very physical time catering to his own strength and agility—a notion that made her stomach flip again, and this time, definitely not in warning.

But it was his face that was the real problem.

He was not a blandly attractive, run of the mill rich guy, like all the rest packed into Deanville at this time of year in their designer ski togs and indistinguishable store-bought tans. Not this man. His face was too relentlessly and uncompromisingly masculine. Too harshly male. He had a nose like an old coin and a hard, stern, unsmiling mouth that made a shocking, impossible heat uncurl, low and insistent, deep in Maggy's belly. If she was honest, lower than that. His gaze was the color of a hard rain and much too shrewd besides. It seemed to kick up some kind of electricity as he aimed it at her, as arrogant and aloof as it was ruthless.

And he stood there with that gray gaze trained on her as if he was used to nothing less than adoration from all he surveyed. As if he expected nothing less from Maggy.

"Who the hell are you?" she demanded. It felt like self-preservation. In that moment, she didn't care if she was fired for her tone. She didn't care if that meant she got behind on the rent of her shabby little room again. She didn't care what happened, as long as the raw, fierce *thing* that swept over her didn't take her down with it.

"That is perfect, of course," the man said, in a dry tone that made it clear that it was no such thing.

"Crude and disrespectful at once. My ancestors turn in their graves as we speak." His voice was rich and deeply cultured, his English spiced by the hint of something else entirely. Maggy loathed the part of her that wanted to know what that *something else* was. Needed to know it, even. The man only gazed down at her, a faint frown marring the granite perfection of his dark, arrogant brow. "Why are you blonde?"

Maggy blinked. Then, worse, lifted a hand to the hair she'd dyed blonde three days ago because she'd decided blonde made her look more approachable than her natural dark chestnut color.

Then she went a little cold as his implication settled deep in her gut.

"Why are you watching me?" she demanded. Not in any sort of approachable manner, because there was friendly and then there was freaked out, and she was already a little too close to the latter. "Are you a stalker?"

There was a slight noise from the goons behind her at the counter, as if they'd reacted to that, but the man before her merely moved one of his index fingers. That was all. He was wearing the sort of buttery soft leather gloves she'd be afraid to touch with her rough hands and he merely lifted one finger. And that was that. Instant silence.

"You do not know who I am."

It wasn't a question. If anything, it seemed like an indictment.

"You do realize," Maggy said slowly, sitting back on her heels and wondering if she could use her bucket and sponge as some kind of weapon if things got serious here, "that anyone who asks that question is basically outing themselves as a giant, irredeemable douche."

His brow rose as if he had never heard the term. But there was no question, as his gray eyes glittered, that he recognized it as the insult it was.

Maggy had the strangest notion he was unused to insults altogether. And perhaps astonished that she dared change that. It meant he was even more of an untouchable rich guy than she'd already imagined— but she couldn't figure out why recognizing that made her a little breathless.

"I beg your pardon." His voice was dark. It rolled through her, making that breathless feeling worse and her chest feel tight besides. "A *douche*? Is that what you called me?"

She tipped her chin up in that way a battalion of counselors and former employers had told her was aggressive, and pretended not to notice the emphasis he put on that last word.

"The coffee shop is closed," she said flatly. "Please gather your goon squad and go and in future? Maybe take a moment or two to consider the fact that marching around with a pack of armed men with potential steroid problems isn't necessary when you're after a cup of coffee."

The man did nothing for a moment but gaze down at her, his dark eyes assessing in a way that washed over her and left strange goose bumps in their wake. Then he thrust his hands into the pockets of his trousers, widening his stance, in a manner that should have looked more casual. But didn't.

"Tell me," he said in that same commanding voice that seemed to resonate deep inside of her. "Do you have a small birthmark behind your left ear? Shaped like a lopsided heart?"

Maggy felt cold. As frigid as the winter air that had rushed inside when they'd arrived.

"No," she said. Though she did. And it took every bit of self-possession she had not to reach up and run her fingers over it.

He only studied her, his austere mouth flat. "You are lying."

"And you're creeping me out," she retorted. She clambered up and onto her feet then, aware again of an instant reaction from the goons—and, again, the way the man in the center stopped them with the faintest wave of one finger. "What is this? What do you want? I'm guessing it's not a Mexi-mocha soy latte with an extra shot."

"Is your name Magdalena, by any chance?"

Maggy understood then that this man already knew the answers to the questions he was asking.

And it hit her like a kick to the belly that he was asking at all. It made the hardwood floors seem to creak and slide beneath her feet.

"No," she lied again. She couldn't have said why she was halfway to panicked, only that she was. "My name is Maggy. It's not short for anything." She pulled her phone from the back pocket of her jeans and clenched it tight in her hand. Maybe she even brandished it at him a little. "And if you don't leave right now, I'm calling the police."

The man didn't smile. His mouth looked as if perhaps he never had. Still, there was a silver gleam to those hard rain eyes of his, and her breath got tangled somewhere in her throat.

"That will be an exercise in frustration for you, I am afraid," he said as if he wasn't the least bit threatened by the notion of the police. Almost as if he welcomed it instead. "If you wish to contact the local authorities, I will not stop you. But it would be remiss of me if I did not warn you that doing so will not achieve the results you imagine."

Maggy couldn't have said why she believed him. But she did. It was something about the way he stood there, as if he was used to being mistaken for a very well-dressed and granite-hewn statue, and was about as soft himself.

"Then how about you just leave?" she asked, aware that her lips felt numb and that her stomach felt…weird, the way it kept flipping and knotting and then twisting some more. And meanwhile that place behind her ear where her birthmark sat seemed to be much too hot. As if it was lit on fire. But she didn't dare touch it. Not in front of this man. "I want you to leave."

But this man in all his haughty, brooding ruthlessness wasn't listening to her. She'd stood up and he was clearly intrigued by that. He let those shrewd gray eyes travel all over her, and the worst part was that she had the childish urge to cover herself while he did it. When really, what did she care if some weird guy stared at her? She didn't wear skinny jeans and tight thermal long-sleeved T-shirts that fit her like a second skin to admire her own figure.

Yet somehow, she got the impression he wasn't staring at her ass like all the other rich guys had when she'd worked down the street in one of the village's bars and they'd been after a little bit of local flavor in between ski runs and highly public divorces.

"It is uncanny," the man said, his voice lower now and something like gruff. "You could be her twin, save the brazenly appalling hair."

"I don't have a twin," Maggy snapped, and she could hear that there was too much *stuff* in her voice then. The way there always was anytime some stranger claimed she looked *just like* their niece or friend or cousin. When she'd been a kid, she'd gotten her hopes up every time. But she was a lot older and whole lot wiser now and she recognized these moments for what they were—throwaway comments from people who had no idea what it was like to have been thrown away themselves. "I don't have anyone, as a matter of fact. I was found by the side of the road when I was eight and I can't remember a single thing from before then. The end."

"Ah, but that only proves my theory," the man said, something hard, like satisfaction, gleaming like silver in those eyes of his.

He pulled off his leather gloves as if it was part of an ancient ceremony. Maggy couldn't have said how he managed it, to somehow exude all of that brooding masculinity and yet be standing there doing nothing but *removing a pair of gloves*. He wasn't sacking the walls of a city or performing some athletic feat, no matter how it echoed around inside of her. When he was done—and when she was busy asking herself what on earth was wrong with her that she should find a man's strong, bare hands *illicit*—he pulled out a smartphone from his pocket, much larger and clearly more high-tech than the one she'd gotten recently when she'd felt so flush after her first month of regular paychecks here. Her fingers clenched hard on hers, as if she was embarrassed by her own phone, and she shoved it in her back pocket again. He swiped his screen a few times and then offered it to her, his face impassive. Though through it all, his gray eyes gleamed.

Maggy stared at his shiny, top-of-the-line smartphone as if it was a wasp's nest, buzzing a warning straight at her.

"I don't want to look at that," she told him. Because he was overwhelming and he didn't make sense and he was *too much*. And she was being smart not to let him reel her into anything, the way she'd always had to be smart, because it was that or be a victim. But that didn't explain the sudden, hollow sensation deep inside her. "I want you to go. Now."

"Look at the picture, please."

He didn't sound as if he was really asking. He didn't sound as if he ever *asked*, come to that. And she noticed he didn't promise that he would leave her alone if she looked as ordered, either.

So Maggy had no idea why she reached out and took the damned smartphone from him, making absolutely certain not to touch him. Or why the faint glint of approval in his stern gray gaze…did something to her. She swallowed hard and looked down at the smartphone in her hand, still warm from its close contact with his skin. Which should absolutely not have made her fight back a shudder.

Maggy focused on the screen in her hand. And then froze.

It was a picture of a woman.

She was standing somewhere beautiful, all gleaming lights and old stone, and she was looking back over one bared shoulder with a wide smile. Her dark chestnut hair was swept back into some kind of complicated bun and she was wearing the sort of dress real people never wore, long and sleek and seemingly threaded through with diamonds to match the bright strands draped around her neck.

If Maggy didn't know better, she'd have said it was a picture of her.

"What is this?" she whispered, aware as she did that her heart was pounding at her. That her stomach knotted so hard it hurt. That her head ached, hard and strange at her temples. "Who *is* this?"

The man before her didn't move a muscle. He didn't lift one of his powerful fingers. He didn't do anything, and yet there was something about the way he watched her then that took over the whole world.

"That is Serena Santa Domini." His voice was cool, and yet she was sure there was something like satisfaction in his voice, threaded in deep, like stone. "Better known as Her Majesty, the queen of Santa Domini, who died twenty years ago in a car crash in Montenegro." His gray eyes flashed with something Maggy didn't understand, dark and sure, but it hit her like a wallop all the same. "I believe she was your mother."

Reza Argos, more widely known and always publicly addressed as His Royal Majesty, King and Supreme Ruler of the Constantines, was not a sentimental man.

That had been his father's downfall. It would not be his.

But either way, there was no doubt that he was a king. That meant there was no room for the maudlin trap of sentiment, especially in a country like the Constantines that prided itself on its *correctness* with, it was true, a certain intensity that suggested a number of unpleasant undercurrents. Like all the whispers about his father's longtime mistress, for example, that no one dared mention directly—especially not after the way his father had died. Not that anyone said *suicide*, either. It was too messy. It hinted too strongly at the darkness beneath the Constantines, and no one wanted that.

It was all unpleasant history. Reza focused on the present. His trains ran on time. His people paid their taxes and his military zealously maintained his borders. He and his government operated transparently, without unnecessary drama, and in the greatest interests of his people to the best of his ability. He did not succumb to the blackmail of a calculating mistress and he certainly did not risk the whole country because of it. He was nothing like his father. More than that, the Constantines were *nothing* like their closest neighbor, the besieged Santa Domini, with its civil and economic crises these last thirty years.

Unsentimental attention to detail on the part of its rulers was how such a small country had maintained its prosperity, independence, and neutrality for hundreds upon hundreds of years. Europe might rage and fall and rise again around them, but the Constantines stood, a firm guard against encroaching darkness and Santa Dominian refugee crises alike, and no matter how grim and worrying it had all been these last three decades.

His father's descent into cringe-inducing protestations of *what the heart demanded*—followed by what might well have become a constitutional crisis had it not been stopped before the blackmail had truly ripped apart the kingdom—did not count. Since very few people knew how bad it had all gotten outside the royal family and the most highly ranked ministers.

Reza had held his tiny alpine country together since his ascension to the throne at the tender age of twenty-three following what had been widely reported as his father's sudden heart attack, as the latest in a long line of monarchs from the House of Argos. The Constantines was a small country made up of two pristine valleys high in the European Alps. The valleys were connected by a vast, crystal blue lake, bristled with picturesque villages and plump, comfortable banking concerns, and were bordered on all sides by crisp snowcapped mountains and luxury ski resorts.

The Constantinian people liked the kingdom as it was. Untouched. A legacy of a bygone era, yet with all the comforts of the present day. That their longtime ally and closest neighbor, Santa Domini, had suffered a violent military coup when Reza was a child, had lost its exiled king and most of its royal family when he was eighteen, and had strewn out refugees seeking escape from the harsh military government all this time made Constantinians…upset.

Reza did not particularly care for the fact that his reign was often characterized as "rocky," purely because he'd had to spend so much of it handling his neighbor's messes and making up for his father's adulterous yearnings, the blackmail that had nearly brought the kingdom to war, and the suicide he'd had no choice but to conceal from the public lest all the rest of it come out, too. He'd handled that necessary lie. He'd handled his furious, spiteful mother. He'd even handled his father's awful mistress. It was unfortunate that no one outside his inner circle knew how much he'd handled. But things were looking up. Next door in Santa Domini, the usurper, General Estes, was dead. The rightful Santa Dominian king's restoration to the throne had changed his country and calmed the whole region.

If this woman in front of him was the lost, long presumed dead Princess Magdalena as he suspected she was, that changed everything else.

Because Reza had been betrothed to the Santa Domini princess since the day of her birth. And while he prided himself on his ability to live without the mawkish sentiment that had brought down his father and led him straight into an unscrupulous woman's hands, he suspected that what his people truly wanted was a convenient royal fairy tale with all the trappings. A grand royal wedding to remind them of their happy fantasies about what life in the Constantines was meant to be was just the ticket. It would generate revenue and interest. It would furthermore lead to the high approval ratings and general satisfaction Reza's grandfather had enjoyed throughout his long reign. Contented subjects, after all, rarely plotted out revolutions.

He opted not to share the happy news with his prospective bride just then.

The woman before him shook slightly as she stared at the picture on his mobile. He'd expected joyful noises, at the very least, as he'd imagined anyone standing in a second-rate resort town undertaking menial labor might make upon learning she was, in all likelihood, meant for greater things than her current dire straits. Or a celebration of some kind, particularly given the circumstances under which he'd found her. On her hands and knees, scrubbing the floor like the lowest servant. Her hair like brittle straw around her bony shoulders, making her look even more pale and skinny than she already was. Wearing the sort of fabrics that looked as if they might set themselves alight if they rubbed together.

Her mouth as foul and crude as the rest of her.

This, then, was his long-lost queen. The fairy-tale creature he would use to beguile his people and secure his throne, all rough, red hands and that sulky, impertinent mouth. He supposed he would have to make the best of it.

And if there was some part of him that was pleased that he could not possibly be in any danger from this creature—that she was about as likely to beguile him as was the exuberant potted plant in the corner—well. He kept that to himself.

She raised her gaze to his again, her eyes a deep, rich caramel that he found he couldn't read as he wished. He watched the curious way she set her frail shoulders and lifted her stubborn chin. As if she wished to hold him off physically. As if she thought she'd have a chance at it if she tried.

On some level, Reza was deeply appalled she might ever have had reason to lift a finger to protect herself. He was almost entirely certain that she was the lost princess of Santa Domini. *His* princess. A blood test would merely confirm what was obvious to the naked eye, as the family resemblance was astonishing. And the lost princess of Santa Domini, the future mother of the kings of the Constantines, was not a scrubbing woman. She was not this… hardscrabble washerwoman persona she'd concocted over the past two decades.

He told himself that he should find it in him to be sympathetic. If he was correct in his assumption about what had happened, she'd been granted a strange mercy indeed—but that made it no less merciful.

"I don't have a mother," she told him, without the faintest shred of deference. Or any hint of manners. And Reza admired her spirit, he supposed, even if he deeply disapproved of its application. "And if I did, she certainly wasn't the queen of anything, unless maybe you mean welfare."

Reza ignored that, already trying to work out how he could possibly take this…fake blonde sow's ear and create the appropriately dignified purse, one worthy of being displayed to the world at his side.

She had the bones of the princess she clearly was. That was obvious at a glance. If he ignored the tragic clothes, the questionable hair, and the decidedly unrefined way she held herself, he could see the stamp of the Santa Dominis all over her. It was those high cheekbones, for a start. The sweet oval of her face and that impossibly lush mouth that was both deeply aristocratic and somehow carnal at once. She was an uncivilized, hungry sort of skinny, a far cry from the preferred whippet-thin and toned physique of the many highborn aristocratic women of Reza's acquaintance, but she was evidently proud of the curves she had. He could imagine no other reason she would have gone to such trouble to wear her cheap clothing two sizes too small.

What Reza could not understand—what curled through him like smoke and horrified him even as it sent heat rushing through him—was how, when he had no worries at all that she could access his heart no matter who she was, he could possibly want her in any way. This…renovation project that stood before him.

And yet.

It had slammed into him the moment he'd walked into the shop and it had appalled him unto the depths of his soul. It still did. He was the king of the Constantines. His tastes were beyond refined, by definition and inclination alike. His mistresses were women of impeccable breeding, impressive education, and all of them were universally lauded for their exquisite beauty, as was only to be expected. Reza did not dabble in shallow pools. He swam deep or not at all.

The woman he'd intended to make his queen, until he'd seen this creature before him now in a photograph ten days ago, was appropriate for him in every possible way. The right background. Unimpeachable bloodlines dating back centuries. An excellent education at all the best schools. A thoughtful, spotless, and blameless career in an appropriate charity following her graduation. Never, ever, so much as a breath of tabloid interest in her or her close friends or anything she did. Not ever.

The honorable Louisa had been the culmination of a decade of hard searching for the perfect queen. He hadn't imagined he'd ever find her until he had. Reza still couldn't entirely believe that he was here, across an ocean from his kingdom and his people and the woman he'd intended to wed, hunting down a crass, ill-dressed creature who had already insulted him in about seventeen different ways. It offended him on every level.

As did the fact that every time she lifted that belligerent chin of hers or opened her mouth to say something indelicate if not outright rude, the most appalling need washed through him and made him… restless.

His Louisa had been crafted as if from a list of his desired specifications for his potential queen, and yet he had never, ever felt anything for her beyond the sort of appreciation for her lovely figure he might also feel for, say, a pretty bit of shrubbery or an elegant table setting. Reza was the king of the Constantines. The state of his garden and the magnificence of his decor reflected on him. On his rule. On his country. So, too, would his choice of bride.

His feelings, appropriately, were that all of these things should be beyond excellence. And that sort of distant admiration was the only feeling he intended to have for his queen, as was appropriate. Unlike his father's disastrous affair of the heart.

"Perhaps you failed to understand me." He waited for the princess's unusual eyes to meet his and gritted his teeth against his body's unseemly reaction to her. It would be one thing if she were dressed like her mother had been in that picture. If she looked like the princess she obviously was instead of a cast-off from *Les Misérables*. What was the matter with him? "Ten days ago my aide returned from a brief location scouting expedition in the area."

"A location scouting expedition." She echoed his own words in much the same way she'd said the word *douche* earlier, and he liked it about as much now as he had then. "Is that fancy talk for *a trip*?"

Reza could not recall the last time any person had managed to get under his skin. Much less a woman. In his experience, women tended to fling themselves into his path with great enthusiasm, if impeccable manners befitting his status, and if they found themselves on their knees, it was for entirely different reasons. He opted not to share that with her. Just as he opted not to share that he'd been planning an engagement trip to ask Louisa to become his queen in appropriately photogenic surroundings. He had not been at all interested in America for this purpose, but his enterprising aide had made a case for the enduring appeal of the New England countryside in winter and the smallish hills they called mountains here.

"I saw you in the background of these pictures." He eyed her brash, blond hair, looking even less attractive in the overhead lights the more she tipped her head back to glare unbecomingly at him. In the pictures her hair had swirled around her shoulders, feminine and enticing, the dark chestnut color suiting her far more. It had also made it abundantly clear whose child she was. "The resemblance to Queen Serena was uncanny. It took only a phone call or two to determine that your name matched that of the lost princess and that your mysterious past dovetailed with the time of the accident. Perfectly. It seems too great a coincidence."

Again, her chin tilted up, and there was no reason at all Reza should feel that as if her hands were on his sex. He was appalled that he did. Until tonight, his desires had always remained firmly under his control. Passion had been his father's weakness. It would not be his.

"I don't have a mysterious past," she told him. Her caramel-colored eyes glittered. "The world is filled with bad parents and disposable kids. I'm just one more."

"You are nothing of the kind."

She folded her arms over her chest in a show of belligerence that made him blink.

"I'll return to my original question," she said. Not politely. "Who the hell are you and why do you care if some barista in a photograph looks like an old, dead queen?"

Reza drew himself up to his full height. He looked down at her with all the authority and consequence that had been pounded into every inch of him, all his life, even when his own father had failed to live up to the crown he now wore himself.

"I am Leopoldo Maximillian Otto, King of the

Constantines," he informed her. "But you may call me by my private family nickname, Reza."

She let out a sharp, hard sound that was not quite a laugh and thrust his mobile back at him. "I don't want to call you anything."

"That will be awkward, then."

Reza took possession of his mobile, studying the way she deliberately kept her fingers from so much as brushing his, as if he was poisonous. When he was a king, not a snake. How this creature dared to treat him—*him*—with such disrespect baffled him, but did nothing to assuage that damnable need that still worked inside him. She confounded him, and he didn't like it.

But that didn't change the facts. Much less what would be gained by presenting his people with the lost Santa Domini princess as his bride.

He met her gaze then. And held it. "Because one way or another, you are to be my wife."

CHAPTER TWO

"I GET IT," Maggy said after a moment. The word *wife* seemed to pound through her like an instant hangover, making her head feel too big and her belly a bit iffy, and if there were other, stranger reactions to him moving around inside her...she pretended she didn't notice. "Someone must have put you up to this. Is this some new reality show? *The Cinderella Games*?"

Reza—as the other six hundred names he'd rattled off, to say nothing of the title he'd claimed, were apparently not fit for daily use—blinked in obvious affront.

"Allow me to assure you that I have not, nor will I ever, participate in a *show* of any kind." He managed to bite out his words as if they offended him. As if the very taste of them in his mouth was an assault. Then he adjusted the cuffs of his coat in short jerks of indignant punctuation. "I am a king, not a circus animal."

Maggy found that despite never having seen a

king in all her life, and having entertained about as many thoughts about the behavior of monarchs as she did about that of unicorns and/or dragons, she had no trouble whatsoever believing this man of stone and consequence was one.

"I'll make a note that you're not a sad, dancing elephant." Somehow, she kept from rolling her eyes in the back of her head. "Good to know."

"I suggest you look it up," he said, very much as if she hadn't spoken. Maybe for him, she really hadn't. It was entirely possible that a king simply wasn't aware that anyone else spoke at all. He nodded toward her hip, and the phone she'd stashed in her back pocket. "Pull up an image of the king of the Constantines on your mobile. See what appears. I think you'll find that he resembles me rather closely."

And Maggy opted not to explore why the certainty in his voice shivered through her, kicking up a commotion in its wake.

"It doesn't matter what comes up," she told him, careful to keep that shivering thing out of her voice. "I don't care if you're the king of the world. I still need to clean this floor and lock up the shop, and that means you and all your muscly clowns need to go." When he only stared at her in cool outrage, she might have smirked a little. Just a little. "You're the one who mentioned a circus. I'm only adding to the visual."

"What an extraordinary reaction." His gray eyes

were fathomless, yet still kicked up entirely too many tornadoes inside of her. And his voice did strange things to her, too. It seemed to echo around inside of her. As if *he* was inside of her—something she was better off not imagining, thank you. "I have told you that it is highly probable you are a member of one of Europe's grand, historic royal families. That you are very likely a princess and will one day become a queen. My queen, no less. And your concern is the floor of a coffee shop?"

"My concern is the lunatic in the coffee shop with me, actually," she managed to say, fighting to keep her voice even. Because she knew, somehow, that if she allowed herself to feel the reaction swelling inside of her, it might take her right back down to her knees. And not by choice this time. "I want you to go."

He studied her for what seemed like a very long time. So long she had to rail at herself to keep from fidgeting. From showing him any weakness whatsoever—or any hint that she was taking him seriously when she wasn't. She couldn't. Princesses? Queens? That was nothing but little girl dreams and wishful thinking.

If there was one thing Maggy knew entirely too much about, it was reality. Cold, hard, grim, and often heartbreaking reality. There was no point whining about it, as she knew very well. It was what it was.

"Very well," he said after what seemed like a thousand years, and was that...*disappointment* that washed through her? Had she wanted him to keep pushing? She couldn't have. Of course she couldn't have. "If you feel you must continue with these unpleasant tasks of yours, then by all means." This time he waved a hand, and it was even more peremptory and obnoxious than his previous partially raised finger. It made her blood feel so hot and so *bright* in her veins that she flushed with it. With temper. And she was certain he saw it. "Don't for one moment allow your bright future to interfere with your menial present circumstances."

Maggy had wanted to hit quite a few people in her time. That was what happened when a girl found herself on her own and entirely alone in the world at eighteen, when the foster care system had spit her out. She'd found herself surrounded by bad people and worse situations in places where violence was the only reasonable response to pretty much anything. Still, she'd scraped by and she'd survived—because what was the alternative?

But she wanted to hit this man more. She even did the math as she eyed him there in front of her. His four goons would likely object to any manhandling of their charge, but she was closer to him than they were. She was sure she could land a satisfying punch before they flattened her. She was equally sure it would be worth the tackle.

She didn't know how she kept her hands to herself.

"I appreciate your permission to do my job." Maggy was not, in fact, anything remotely like appreciative. "Here's a newsflash. Even if you are a king, you aren't *my* king."

She watched, fascinated despite herself, as a muscle worked in his granite-hewn jaw, indicating the impossible. That this man of stone and regal airs was having his own set of reactions to her.

To *her*.

There was absolutely no reason she should feel that as some kind of victory when she didn't *want* to win this. Whatever this was.

"You will dine with me tonight," he told her, in the manner of one who was used to issuing proclamations and, more, having them instantly obeyed.

Maggy let out a short, hard laugh. "Um, no. I won't be doing that. Tonight or ever."

Reza only gazed back at her, and she told herself she was imagining that little suggestion of heat in his stern gaze. That she was a crazy woman for imagining it. That he was a *king*, for God's sake. That she shouldn't care either way, because it was her own, personal law that she didn't do complications of any kind.

And there was no pretending a man who pranced around calling himself a king in a coffee shop wasn't one giant complication, no matter how harshly compelling that fierce face of his was.

"Then I am happy to remain where I am," he told her after another long, tense moment.

"Until what?" She shook her head, then shoved a chunk of her hair back behind her ear. "You convince me that this insane story is true? I already know it isn't. Princesses don't go missing and end up in foster care no matter how many little girls wish they did. You're wasting your time."

"You cannot possibly know that until you take a blood test."

"Oh, a blood test? Is that all?" Maggy bared her teeth at him. "You can expect *that* to happen over my dead body."

He smiled then. And it was devastating. It…did things to his face. Made it something far closer to beautiful than any man so hard and uncompromising should ever look. It should have been impossible. It was certainly unfair. Maggy's mouth went dry. Parts of her body she'd stopped paying any attention to outside of their sheer biological functions prickled to uncomfortable awareness.

Oh, no, she thought.

"Let me tell you how this will go," Reza said softly, as if he knew exactly what was happening to her. As if he was pleased it was. "You will give me a blood sample. You will sit and eat a decent dinner with me tonight not only because I wish to get to know you, but because you look as if you haven't eaten well in some time. If ever. The blood test will

confirm what I already know, which is that you are
Her Royal Highness Magdalena of Santa Domini.
At which point, you will leave this menial existence
that is beneath you in more ways than it is possible
to number and is an insult to the blood in your veins.
And then, among other things, you will assume your
rightful position in your brother's court and in the
line of ascension to his throne."

She'd opened her mouth to protest his snide reference to her menial life, not to mention his idea that
she was some wayward waif who'd never eaten a
meal, but got caught on that last bit.

Maggy's heart seemed to twist in her chest. "My
brother?"

And she knew she gave herself away with that.
There was no chance this overwhelming man didn't
hear the breathiness in her voice. The longing for
that life so many people took for granted. A life with
family. With *people* who were as much hers as she
was theirs, whatever that looked like. The kind of
life she'd never had—and had taught herself a long
time ago to stop wishing for.

"Yes," Reza said. His harshly regal head canted
to one side, though he kept his gaze on hers. "Your
brother. He is the king of Santa Domini. Previous to
his coronation, he was rather well-known as one of
the world's greatest and most scandalous playboys.
If you have been in the vicinity of a tabloid news-
paper over the past twenty years, you will have seen

a great deal of him, I'd imagine. Too much of him, I would wager."

Her hands felt numb. With some distant part of her brain, it occurred to her to think that was a strange reaction. That pins and needles should stab at her fingers as if her arms had fallen asleep when they hadn't. When, despite what was happening here, she was very much awake.

"Cairo," Maggy whispered. Because even she knew that name. Everybody knew that name. She'd seen his pictures all over every magazine in existence for as long as she could remember, because there was nothing else to do while standing in line in sad discount supermarkets stocking up on cheap staples but look at pretty people doing marvelous things in exotic places. "Cairo Santa Domini."

Reza inclined his head. "The one and only. He is your brother. As someone who saw him in person not long ago and is now looking at you, I must tell you that there is absolutely no doubt that you are his blood relative."

Maggy shook her head. She took a step back and only stopped because she had nowhere to go, with his henchmen looming back near the counter. "No."

She didn't know what she was denying. Which part of this madness. Only that it was crucial to her sanity—to everything that had kept her upright and grimly moving forward all her life no matter what got thrown at her—that she keep doing so.

But his dark gaze was much too knowing on hers. She was sure he could see far too much. And the fact he could—that he seemed to have no problem whatsoever seeing straight through her when no one else had ever come close—shook through her like a winter storm, treacherous and dark.

"This will not go away, Princess," he told her, very matter-of-factly. And he didn't shift that gaze of his from hers. "Nor will I. And you can be certain that if I recognized you, so, too, will someone else."

"I think you're overestimating the amount of time people in your world spend looking closely at people in mine."

Again, a curve of those stern lips, and she wasn't equipped to deal with that. She couldn't process it. She could only feel the way it flushed over her, like another kick of temper when she knew full well it wasn't that. She might not have felt anything like it in recent memory, but she knew it wasn't anything close to *temper*.

"You're decades too late," she threw at him. She didn't know where it came from. Or, worse, she knew exactly where it came from. That dark little hollow place she carried around inside of her that nothing ever filled. And she couldn't seem to stop herself once she'd started. "Everyone dreams they're secretly a princess when they're ten. Especially in foster care. But I'm over that now. This is my life. I made it, I'm happy with it, and I'm staying in it."

"Come to dinner with me anyway," he ordered her, and there was something about the way he said things as if they were laws instead of requests that, oddly, made her want to obey him. She had to lock her knees to keep from moving toward him. She, who was famous for her attitude problems and inability to follow the orders of people who were *paying* her to listen to them. What was *that*? "You can consider it a date."

Maggy assumed he was joking. Because he had to be joking, of course. No one asked her for dates, even roundabout ones like this one. She had *stay the hell away from me* stamped all over her face, she was pretty sure.

And the few times anyone had actually mustered up all their courage and asked that scrappy Strafford girl on a date, it had not been a king.

Not that she'd independently verified this man was who he said he was.

"I would rather die than go on a date with you," she told him, which was melodramatic and also, in that moment, the absolute truth.

Again that slow, coolly astonished blink of his, as if he required extra time to process what she'd said to him—and not, she was quite sure, because he didn't understand her.

"How much money can you possibly make in this place?" he asked.

"That's rude. And it's none of your business. Just

like everything else about me is none of your business. You don't get to know everything about another person simply because you demand it or send your little minions to dig it up."

"By minions, am I to assume you mean my staff?"

"If you want to know things about someone, you ask. You wait to see if they answer. If they don't, it could be because they don't want to answer you because your question is obnoxious. Or because they think you're a random creepy guy who showed up with his personal collection of armed men after closing time to say a whole lot of crazy things, suggesting you might be delusional. Or that you won't go away no matter what you are. Or in my case, all of the above."

That muscle in his jaw clenched tight. "Consider dinner with me an employment opportunity." When she only stared back at him, that muscle clenched tighter. "An interview for a position, if you will."

"A position as what? Your next little piece on the side? While I'm sure competition for that downward spiral is intense, I'll pass. I prefer my lovers, you know, *sane*."

She knew she'd gone too far then. Reza went very, very still. His gray eyes seemed to burn through her. Her pulse took off at a gallop and she had to order herself to keep breathing.

"Be very careful, Magdalena," he advised her,

his voice low and stern and still, it wound its way through her like a wicked heat. "I have so far tolerated your impudence because it is clear you cannot help yourself, given your circumstances. But you begin to stray too far into the sort of insults that cannot and will not be tolerated. Do you understand me?"

Maggy understood that he was far more intimidating than he should have been, and she was fairly hard to cow. She told herself it didn't matter. That she was as numb as she wished she really was, head to toe, except for that wildness deep in her core that she wanted to deny was there.

She rolled her eyes. "You don't have to worry about tolerating me. And I really don't care if you do or don't. What you do have to do is go."

He let out a breath, but she knew, somehow, he wasn't any less furious.

"I have already told you the only way that will happen and I am not in the habit of repeating myself. Nor am I renowned for going back on my word. Two things you would do well to keep in mind."

And Maggy thought, to her horror, that she might explode. And worse, do it right in front of him. Something was rolling inside of her, heavy and gathering steam, and she was terrified that she might break down in front of this granite wall of a man and humiliate herself. *Ruin* herself.

She didn't know him. She didn't *want* to know

him. But she knew, beyond a shadow of a doubt, that she couldn't show any weakness in front of him or it would kill her.

"Fine," she gritted out at him, because when there were no more defensive plays to make, offense was the only way to go. She'd learned that the hard way, too, like everything else. "I'll have dinner with you. But only if you leave right now."

And then she wished she could snatch the words back the moment she'd said them.

Reza didn't smile or gloat. He didn't let that stark, hard mouth of his soften at all. And yet there was that silver gleam in his gaze that kicked at her anyway and was worse, somehow, than the gloating of a lesser man. Or it hit her harder, anyway.

He merely inclined his head. Then he named the fanciest resort within a hundred-mile radius, waiting until she nodded.

"Yes," she bit out, letting her sharpness take over her tone because it was much, much better than what she was afraid hid beneath it. "I know where it is."

"I will expect you in one hour," he told her.

Expect away, idiot, she thought darkly.

But she made herself smile. "Sure thing."

"And if you do not appear," Reza said quietly, because apparently he really could read her like a very simple book, "I will come and find you. I know where you live. I know where you work. I know the car you drive, if, indeed, that deathtrap can rightly be called a car at all. I have an entire security force at my beck and call, and as the sovereign of another nation, even one who is flying under the radar as I am here, I am granted vast diplomatic immunity to do as I please. I would suggest you consider these things carefully before you imagine you can plot your way out of this."

And he turned on his heel before she could come up with a response to that. Which was good, because she didn't have one. His men leapt to serve him, flanking him and opening the door for him, then swept him back out into the night.

The cold air rushed in again. The door slapped shut behind him, the echo of the bell still in the air.

Maggy was breathing too hard. Too loud. And she couldn't seem to operate her limbs.

So she made herself move. She sank back down to her knees and she scrubbed that damned sticky area like her life depended on it. And only when she was finished, only when she'd mopped the rest of the floor and dealt with her bucket in the utility room in the back, did she pull out her own phone again.

She looked at it for a long moment. Maybe too long.

Then she pretended she was doing something, anything else as she opened up her browser and typed in *king of the Constantines*...

And there he was. Splashed all over the internet. On the covers of reputed newspapers and all over their inside pages. In image after image. She saw articles about his childhood. His education at Cambridge. His coronation following his father's sudden heart attack and the war he'd wrenched his country back from in the months that followed. That same harsh face. That same arrogant brow. That same imperial hand waving here, there, everywhere as he gave orders and addresses and spoke of this law and that moral imperative and the role of the monarchy in the modern world.

It was him. Reza was exactly who he'd said he was.

Which meant that there was a very high probability that she was, too.

And this time, when Maggy went back down on her knees on the floor, it wasn't because she was in a hurry to get back to cleaning it.

It was because for the first time in her entire life, when she'd learned how to be tougher than tough no matter what, her knees failed to hold her.

CHAPTER THREE

By the time Maggy walked into the gaspingly precious and markedly high-class resort and spa, set in all its grand timber and soaring glass splendor some miles outside of Deanville at the foot of the local mountains, she'd done a great deal more research.

She'd gone home after locking up the coffee shop and she'd crouched there on her single bed in her narrow little room with her phone to her face, taking an internet crash course on the life and times of the Santa Domini royal family. And everything she'd discovered had made her...a little bit dizzy.

Could this be real? Could she have a history after all these years of being nothing but a blank slate? Would she finally discover how and why she'd been left by the side of that road twenty years ago? Was it possible that the answer really, truly was something like one of the many silly and fanciful stories she'd made up when she was a girl to explain it away?

She'd spent a lot of time and energy back then trying to explain to herself how and why she'd ended up the way she had. The possibility that she'd been a kidnapped princess had featured heavily in the rotation of the tales she'd told herself when she'd still had a little foolish hope left. After all, it was a much better story than the more likely one—that whatever adults had been responsible for her had abandoned her because they couldn't care for her or didn't want that kind of commitment any longer. For whatever depressing reasons adults would have to make such decisions. A few came to mind as more likely than finding out she was a misplaced princess. Substance abuse, for example. Mental illness. Poverty. She could take her pick and they all ended the same way: a sad eight-year-old girl on the side of a road with no memory of how she'd gotten there.

But that wasn't the sort of story Maggy had wanted to tell herself back then. Princesses won hands down every time.

"Don't get your hopes up," she'd snapped at herself, there in her rented room in an old, converted Victorian that had likely seen its better days when Vermont was still more or less one big farm.

She'd scrolled through pictures of the queen, the king. She'd taken great care not to think the word *parents*. Or the other, more personal words that indicated the kind of close relationships she'd never had with anyone. *Mother. Father.* And she'd sucked up her courage and taken a long, close look at the princess who had supposedly died in that car accident twenty years ago. She'd stared at that little girl's face, not sure what she saw when she looked at it. Or what, if anything, she *should* see. There was no sense of recognition. There was…nothing inside of her. No spark, no reaction. There was simply the picture of a little girl lost years ago.

And then she'd studied the many, many pictures of and corresponding articles about Cairo Santa Domini. He was once the most scandal-prone royal in all of Europe. Now he was the beloved king of the country he'd taken back from the military everyone seemed to assume had not only wrested control of his kingdom thirty years ago, but ten years after that had engineered that car accident in Montenegro to take out the exiled king. And in so doing, had killed everyone in the Santa Domini royal family save King Cairo himself, who had been in boarding school in the United States at the time.

He was potentially her only living family member.

It was possible, after all this time and a life lived entirely on her own in every conceivable way, that she *actually had* a living family member.

Maggy had felt as if she might be sick.

She'd thought a lot about simply getting into her junky old car and driving absolutely anywhere Reza—who it seemed really was the king he'd claimed he was no matter how little she wanted that to be true—was not.

But in the end, she hadn't done it. She'd thrown

on the only dress she owned that was even slightly nice and she hadn't gone to too much trouble with the rest because he'd made his feelings about her appearance pretty clear. And then she'd driven herself over to the upscale resort instead of out west toward California. And yes, she had to sit in her car in the frigid parking lot until her hands stopped shaking, but that was between her and her steering wheel and the close, hard dark all around.

Maggy prided herself on the toughness she'd earned every day of the past twenty years, having had no one to depend on but herself. Ever. That meant that no matter how she felt—in this case, about as far from *tough* as it was possible to get without actually dissolving into a sea of tears, which she never allowed herself and certainly not in public places— she'd pulled herself together and climbed out of that car, her shaking hands be damned. She'd wanted answers to questions she'd stopped asking years ago. It was a little bit surprising *how very much* she wanted them, so long after she'd decided wondering about such things only made her weak. And how, with only the slightest provocation—if that was what she could call the appearance of an actual king in The Coffee Queen on Main Street—all those same old questions flooded her.

Making her realize she'd never really gotten over wondering who she was or where she'd come from the way she'd assured herself she had. She'd simply stuffed her urge to ask those things way down deep inside, where none of that could leak out into her daily life any longer. The way it had when she'd been much younger and much, much angrier about her lot in life.

When she started across the chilly, icy parking lot, well salted to make certain the wealthy people who could afford to stay here didn't slip, break their heads open, and then fail to pay their astronomical bills, she was caught for a moment in the dark grip of the cold night. It seemed to tumble down around her and she took as deep a breath as she could stand of the sharp winter air, tipping her head back so she could see all the far-off stars gleaming there above her.

Always watching. Always quiet, always calm. No matter what darkness was engulfing her, the stars shone through.

By the time Maggy made it to the front door of the resort, that great, raw thing inside of her that felt like the sort of sob that she'd rather die than let free had subsided a bit. Just a bit. But it was enough to keep her hands from shaking.

A hotel employee with a clipboard and a walkie-talkie waited for her in the slick, self-consciously rustic lobby of the hotel, a serene smile on her face, as if she and Maggy had already met a thousand times before. Maggy was certain they had not.

"If you'll follow me, Ms. Strafford," the woman said warmly. Maybe too warmly, Maggy thought, when greeting a complete stranger. "I'll take you where you need to go. Mr. Argos—" and there was specific emphasis on that name "—is waiting."

On any other night Maggy would have asked a few follow-up questions. Demanded to know how this woman knew who she was at a glance, for a start. But something told her she didn't want to know the answer to that question. That it would involve the word *appalling* again. And while Maggy felt her self-esteem was strong enough to withstand the snotty comments of an uninvited king in her coffee shop, there was no point testing that theory here, in the sort of five-star hotel broke girls like herself normally gave a wide berth.

Instead, she let the woman lead her back outside and into a waiting hotel shuttle, clearly set aside for her use. She didn't ask any questions then, either. She only settled into the seat she was offered in the otherwise empty vehicle and stared out the window, trying to keep her eyes on the stars as the shuttle wound its way out into the depths of the property, deep into the woods and halfway up the mountain. It stopped there. Maggy glanced out to see a guard-house and gates, and heard many short bursts of noise on multiple walkie-talkies before the shuttle started to move again.

"It's only a few moments more," the woman from the hotel told her, still smiling so happily.

Maggy practiced smiling like a normal person. It was a skill she'd never mastered, given how little

cause she'd had to go around smiling at random people. Or at all. In her experience, anyone who wanted
her to *act friendly* and who wasn't paying her to do
so was best avoided altogether. It felt awkward and
wrong, as if she was *doing something* to her cheeks.
She was relieved when the woman looked back to
the shuttle driver instead.

Gradually, Maggy realized they were on a long
driveway. It climbed farther up the steep incline in
a corridor of evergreens and ghostly birch trees,
then stopped beneath a towering palace of a house
done in more timber and even more dramatic glass.
It sprawled over the mountainside as if it had been
placed there by divine intervention instead of the
resort's developers.

She wasn't the least bit surprised that this was
where Reza was staying.

And when she walked inside the soaring entry hall
that must have commanded views over most of New
England in the sunlight, she was equally unsurprised
to find a battalion of servants waiting for her as if
she'd strolled into Buckingham Palace.

Not that she'd ever been anywhere near Buckingham Palace. But she'd seen as many pictures of
the British palace in the supermarket tabloids over
the years as she had of Cairo Santa Domini and his
exploits.

After her coat was taken and she'd been greeted
approximately nine hundred times by uniformed

staff members who pledged to attend to her every need, whatever those might be, Maggy was led off into the house. Each room she walked through was more impressive than the last. Here a library of floor-to-ceiling books and dark leather armchairs pulled close to a crackling fire. There what appeared to be a games room, with a pool table and a chess table and stout cupboards likely filled with every board game imaginable, if she'd had to guess. A large living area, ripe with comfortable couches and deep, thick rugs set out before the glass windows and an outside deck with views over the valley. A closer, more intimate den, with wide armchairs and enveloping sofas and the sort of wall of closed wood cupboards she figured hid television equipment.

Only when she'd walked for what seemed like miles was she finally delivered into a final room. This one was as magnificent as the rest. It featured cozy log walls and architecturally significant windows. There was a stone fireplace and a small seating area arranged around it, and in the center of that area stood a small table set for two.

Maggy stared at that intimate little setup for so long, her heart doing strange things in the back of her throat, she forgot to look around at the rest of the room.

"Do not tell me you have never seen a dinner table before."

His voice was dark and perhaps slightly amused.

She jerked her head away from the table and the fire and there he was, standing near a small, personal bar, where he'd clearly just poured himself a drink.

Reza Argos. His Royal Majesty, the king of the Constantines.

Her heart went wild. She felt her pulse rocket through her, making her strangely aware of her temples, her neck. Her wrists. Her sex. Her hands felt numb again, and twice as shaky, and she couldn't tell if it was the insane circumstances or if it was just him. His gaze was gray and steady on her, and that made it worse. That made it…dangerous in ways she was afraid to consider too closely.

It had been one thing when she'd thought he was a crazy person, there in the coffee shop. It had been easy to keep her wits about her. But now she knew who he was. And that seemed to make everything feel…precarious.

"They buried that princess," she blurted out.

Because if she waited, she was afraid she wouldn't dare ask. She was afraid of too many things, suddenly, and they all had to do with his harshly fierce face and those elegant hands. And the truth was that she *wanted things*—and that, more than anything else, made her chest feel tight and jittery. Maggy hadn't made it this far by wanting things she couldn't have. She'd learned better. And yet here she was anyway.

"With her parents," she continued when Reza only gazed back at her, his gray eyes glittering as if he was trying to read her. "I can't possibly be a person whose body was recovered from an accident site, legally identified, and then very publicly laid to rest. No one can, but especially not some random foster care kid on the other side of the world."

"A very good evening to you, too." His dark voice was reproving. And something else that moved in her, deep and low.

Maggy told herself she could not possibly have cared less what *moved in her*. And that she shouldn't feel it—or anything—anyway.

"Oh, I'm sorry," she said. Or really *seethed*. "Did you think I was here for my health? You told me a huge, ridiculous fairy tale of a story earlier. If it's the lie it seems to be, I'm out of here."

Reza swirled the amber liquid in his crystal tumbler and eyed her over the top of it.

"*A* body was found, yes," he said, his tone cool. "It was said to be the princess's, but then, the entire royal family was identified by members of the very military who had ousted them. There is no telling who lies in those graves. But until now, aside from a few conspiracy theorists in dark corners of the internet, no one had any reason to doubt it was exactly who General Estes's government said it was."

"So in this conspiracy theory, the king and queen are alive, too?" Maggy did nothing to keep that scoffing note out of her voice. "And, what—are currently wandering around aimlessly, disguised as homeless people in Topeka?"

His regal brow rose in affronted astonishment. Or whatever the kingly version of that was, and what pricked at Maggy was that she felt that, too. Everywhere, as if his expression was specially calibrated to work inside her like a flush of heat. She shoved that weirdness aside.

"Topeka?" he echoed. As if she'd said *chlamydia*.

"It's a city. In Kansas."

Reza blinked. Very slowly. She understood that it was deliberate. It was how he indicated his displeasure. That, too, made her feel entirely too warm.

"And Kansas is one of your states, is it not?"

She practiced her smile. "Do you need me to give you a geography lesson?"

He didn't quite sigh. He seemed to grow taller and stormier at the same time, and somehow more formidable. He was wearing a dark suit that was unlike any suit she'd ever seen a man wear in her life. Calling it a *suit* seemed like an insult. It was molded to his tall, solid form, *doing things* to his broad shoulders and making it impossible to look away from all his lean, hard muscles and the planes of his well-cut chest.

"I understand that I must treat you as I would any stray, wild creature I happened upon," he said, almost musingly, his voice calm and light, though his hard gaze gleamed silver. "Your instinct is to bite first. It is no doubt how you survived this ordeal unscathed."

His gaze swept over her, from the top of her head where she'd clipped back her hair in what even she knew was a sad attempt at the sort of hairstyles she'd seen the queen wearing in those pictures to her shoes, which were the black stiletto heels she'd been required to wear during her brief tenure as a cocktail waitress last year. His gaze rose again, taking in every detail of her stretchy little black dress and making her feel as if she was stripped naked, before he found her gaze again.

"Relatively unscathed, that is," he amended.

And that was a different kind of heat then. The scorching reaction to the way he looked at her and then the slap of the insult. Maggy hated both versions. She had to order herself not to clench her fists. Not because she didn't want to hit him; she did. But because she didn't want him to have the slightest idea how much he got to her.

She had no idea how or why she knew that would be the death of her. Only that it would. And that she had to do whatever she could to avoid it.

"Two things," she managed to say, keeping the various rioting factions inside of her at bay and her voice as chilly as the winter night pressing against the windows. "First, I'm not a raccoon. It might surprise you to learn that I don't really like being compared to one. And second, is an insult called something different when it comes out of the mouth of a king?"

His mouth pressed into a hard line, and he set his glass down on the bar with a sharp *click*. He crossed the room in an easy step or two, which wasn't an improvement because then he was *right there*. Too solid. Too tall. And much too close.

He gazed down at her, his gray eyes like a storm, and she couldn't understand that. Why *he* seemed as if this was hard for *him* when it had so little to do with him. He was a messenger, nothing more. He wasn't the one who'd been discarded.

You don't know that you are, either, she snapped at herself.

But then everything stopped. Inside her. Out in the world. Everywhere.

Because he reached out his hand and he touched her.

He touched her.

He fit his hand to her cheek gently. Very gently. As touches went, it was innocuous. Maggy had fended off far more intimate grabs at her person as a matter of course when she'd worked in that cocktail bar.

But this was Reza.

And everything changed.

His palm was hot. Hard. It molded to her jaw while his fingers brushed into her hair, then ran over that spot behind her ear where her birthmark lay. As if he knew exactly where it was. As if he knew exactly who she was. And something burst open inside of her. She'd never felt anything like it. It exploded wide-open, then rolled through her, sensation rocketing from her cheek to her limbs. She felt herself shake. Worse, she knew he could feel it.

She told herself to jerk away from him. But she didn't. She couldn't.

Her eyes were too wide. His were too gray.

"It is called an insult either way," he said quietly, and she thought she heard an echo of that impossible explosion in his dark voice. She was sure of it when he dropped his hand and adjusted the cuff of his jacket and the crisp white shirt beneath it. "But most people, of course, would pretend it was a bit of flattery instead, simply because it came from me."

What Maggy wanted to pretend was that her heart wasn't racing. That the lopsided heart behind her ear didn't seem to burn like a brand because he'd touched it. That she didn't feel trembling and silly and ridiculously vulnerable. That there wasn't that ominous prickling behind her eyes, and that deep in her core, she wasn't melting and much too soft.

But she couldn't quite get there. She took a deep breath instead.

"It must be nice to be king," Maggy said after a moment, and the funny thing was that there was no edge in her voice then. As if she'd forgotten to try to play the angles here. As if his touch had smoothed them all away, making her feel safe when she knew she wasn't.

"I bet no one tells *you* that you need to modify your tone and attitude or you'll be out of a job."

His lips quirked. "Certainly not. No one would dare."

And suddenly, Maggy didn't care if she looked weak. She needed to put space between them. She needed to keep his hands away from her, because she didn't know what she might do with her own. She stepped back and she didn't care how silver that gleam in his eyes was.

"Come," he said then, and she didn't like that. The way his voice was so rich and warm, as if it was as much a part of the fire that crackled in the stone fireplace as it was of him.

Get a grip, she ordered herself.

He ushered her to one of the seats at that intimate table before the fire then, and everything got awkward as he held her seat. Or maybe she was the awkward thing here, while she could still feel his hand against her skin like a new tattoo, a red-hot pulse of sensation. She didn't let herself look at him. She sat down and was *aware* of him all around her, looming and compelling, as he pushed her closer to the table. It was such an odd, old-world sort of gesture, she thought as he took the seat opposite her. There was no reason at all she should feel so…fluttery.

She was absurdly glad that there was now a table between them.

As if responding to some secret signal, a breath

after Reza sat down the doors to the room opened and their dinner was wheeled in by more uniformed servants. As they bustled about the table, a different man appeared at her side. This one wore a dark suit and a diffident smile, and held what looked like medical supplies in his hands.

"If I could take a quick sample, Ms. Strafford," he murmured, but his gaze was on the king.

Maggy's eyes flew to Reza's. Too much silver and too much hard gray beneath it. Yet Reza only gazed back at her, his mouth an unsmiling line.

"Do you want to know?" he asked quietly. "I think you already suspect the truth. I know I do. But this is how we know for certain."

That question echoed inside of her like a drum, loud and low and long.

Did she want to know? He'd offered her this lovely little fairy-tale explanation for her life earlier this evening. A mere handful of hours ago. But she'd risen to meet it, armed with twenty years of her own secret fairy tales to choose from, rattling around inside of her and making all of this feel a whole lot more fraught with peril and meaning than it should.

Do you want to know?

Maggy told herself—sternly—that she wanted to confirm the fact that she was not Magdalena Santa Domini. That the only reason she was here was to prove him wrong, and it had nothing at all to do with that scraped-raw hollow deep inside her, that unleashed sob she refused to let out. That it had nothing to do with a lost little girl, tossed aside like so much trash, who had waited her whole life to belong somewhere.

That she was not a fairy-tale princess. That she'd gotten over imagining otherwise a long time ago. That there was nothing wrong with reality and who cared that once upon a time she'd wet her pillows every night with too many tears for too many fantastical stories that never came true.

She told herself she'd exorcised that little girl a long time ago. And that this, right here, was a way to make sure she never came back—because that little girl was dangerous. She didn't know any better than to *want* with abandon.

Maggy refused to meet Reza's gaze then. She ignored the little voice inside of her that warned her not to do this, no matter what might come of it. And then she held out her arm and let the smooth-faced man draw a vial of her blood, as quickly and efficiently as the other servants tended to the plating and presentation of the food.

That was it, then, she thought as the man gathered up his supplies, bowed slightly to the king, and took his leave. The answer was coming at her whether she liked it or not. Like a train.

"When will we know?" she asked. Despite her best attempt to keep from saying anything.

"Shortly." Reza's gaze was still on her, she could

feel it. She kept hers on the edge of her heavy silver fork. More precisely, *one of* her heavy silver forks. "I've assembled a makeshift laboratory in the solarium."

That didn't surprise her at all. "Of course you have."

Maggy stared down at her plate as a first course was set there before her, not sure what it was and also not at all sure she could eat anything anyway. She told herself that was what happened when she had a needle stuck in her body three seconds before dinner, but she was fooling no one with that, least of all herself. She felt…outside herself. Turned inside out. Exposed in a way that didn't make sense, when this man had no more idea who she really was than she ever had.

The feeling only got worse when the staff retreated, leaving them alone in a bright little room that seemed to shrink tight around them.

"It is a country paté," Reza murmured, sounding remote and polite. As if he was commenting on the weather. "Locally sourced, I imagine."

Maggy blinked at her plate, then at him. And knew before she opened her mouth that she shouldn't. That there were too many vast, unwieldy things rocking around inside of her and making her…not quite herself. But that didn't stop her.

"I don't understand the point of this. You said you wanted to get to know me, which we both know isn't true. You don't want to know *me*. You have some fantasy about a lost princess. And I didn't agree to eat—" she wrinkled up her nose "—whatever this is."

"Your palate is likely far more refined, I am sure."

"My palate is basically Cheetos and beer," she retorted, which wasn't exactly true. She also enjoyed ramen. "Does that dilute royal blood? If so, I'm afraid you're not going to get the answer you want."

She had the impression he was clenching his teeth again, though she couldn't actually see it. Only that same muscle in his freshly shaved jaw, calling attention to the harsh perfection of his decidedly regal face.

But when he spoke, his voice was smooth. Calm. "I notice that you seem to have accepted both that I am the king I claimed I was and that you, too, might indeed be Magdalena Santa Domini."

Maggy wouldn't have called the feelings sloshing around inside of her just then *acceptance*. She shrugged, hoping to mask them a little.

"You're either the king of the Constantines or a very good impersonator," she told him offhandedly. "And I'm not sure an impersonator would go to the trouble or expense of renting out this ridiculous place for the sole purpose of conning a broke coffee shop barista." She considered that a moment. "I can't see any reason why anyone would bother conning me."

Again, she saw that mix of affront and astonishment all over his regal face.

"I am delighted that I have distinguished myself in some way from those charming individuals who clamber about in places like Times Square, dressed up as some or other famous fictional character. For tips." He cut something on his plate, too precisely, as if *tips* was a filthy curse word. But then he looked at her instead of putting his food into his mouth, and she had the impression that edge in his voice made a far better knife than the one he held. In that hand of his she could still feel on her jaw. "The generations of monarchs who preceded me to the throne of the Constantines would no doubt be pleased that a son of the House of Argos has not been mistaken for a street corner hustler with a traveling act."

Maggy felt as if she was sitting on an earthquake, not a chair with a high, solid back. As if the more she pretended the whole planet wasn't shaking there, directly underneath her, the more it actually tore through her, shifting whole continents and ripping up the ground.

"I don't want to talk about country paté or my clothes or wild animals," she managed to say, her voice as edgy as his had been, if somewhat less precise. "You said a lot of things in the coffee shop today."

"I did."

"What happens..."

"Eyes on me, if you please. Not your plate."

Her gaze rose and met his of its own accord. As if she had nothing to do with it—because if left to her own devices, Maggy knew she would have ignored that order. Especially when she was lost in all that intent gray, focused on her as if nothing else existed.

And she couldn't believe she was going to ask the question. She couldn't believe that after all this time she was going to take so little care of herself when it most mattered—when she most needed to protect what little was left of her that could still be hurt. But she couldn't seem to keep herself from it.

"What happens if the blood test says what you think it will?" she asked, because she couldn't seem to help it.

And once again, she could see intense satisfaction all over him. It made him seem bigger. Harder. More dangerous than she thought a king ought to seem, especially when he wasn't doing anything but sitting there on the other side of a few fresh flowers and a couple of dramatic candles.

"Once your identity is verified it becomes a question of how and when to announce yourself to the world."

"You mean to Cairo Santa Domini." She frowned at him when he didn't respond, though he kept that hard, intent gaze of his trained on her. "Surely you would tell him first. If it turns out he's actually…" She couldn't say the word. But then she worried not saying it was more telling, so she forced it out, ignoring how it felt in her mouth. "If he's family."

"Of course," Reza said after a moment, but she wasn't sure she believed him. "But there are one or two matters to attend to before placing you in the spotlight your brother seems to roll around with him wherever he goes. It is a very bright spotlight, I must tell you, the sort that brings all manner of things out from the shadows. It is a decidedly relentless glare."

Maggy couldn't bring herself to worry about spotlights, of all things. She thought Reza meant that figuratively, but who knew? He was a real, live king. Cairo Santa Domini was also a real, live king. For all she knew, real, live kings traveled with actual physical spotlights wherever they went, as part of their entourages.

She concentrated on the other part. "Matters? What matters?"

Reza leaned back in his chair and studied her for a moment. She was caught by the forearm he'd left on the table, strong and hard, a hint of the excessively masculine watch he wore peeking out from his cuff. It was outfitted with enough inset gadgetry to man a space shuttle, she thought. Or, hell, operate a spotlight or two if he needed one.

"I do not wish to insult you, Magdelena."

"Maggy," she corrected him, but without the heat she should have summoned, mostly because she… liked that version of her name in his mouth. *Any* version of her name, for that matter.

Idiot.

He appeared not to hear her anyway. "But the fact remains that you have spent the past twenty years in a situation that can only be called some-what suboptimal."

"I can think of a whole lot of other things to call my 'situation.'" She let out a short laugh. "None of them polite."

He inclined his head in that way of his that made her want to scream. And also maybe reach her own hand out, across the table, and touch his.

Obviously, she did nothing of the kind. Because that was *insane*.

"You will be the subject of intense scrutiny." He tapped one of his long, tapered fingers against the tabletop, as if to a beat in his head only he could hear. "It will make the coverage of your brother all these years seem mild in comparison. You cannot under-estimate the draw such a story will have."

Maggy tried out one of those smiles again. "Every-body likes a princess."

"But that is the issue, of course." His stern mouth curved slightly, and she had the strangest notion that he was trying to be kind. "Not everyone will, and not in the same way. Particularly not a long-lost princess who has suddenly emerged fully grown to claim her place in the world with all its attendant privileges. And those who do not care for a princess who rises from the dead will attack you however they can. They will dig into your life here. They will rip you to shreds in the papers. They will use any ammuni-tion they can find to shame you."

"Why?"

His gaze was matter-of-fact. "Because they can. Because they are paparazzi scum who love nothing more than tearing things down however possible. Because it sells." He shrugged. "You can pick any reason you like, but the manipulation of public sentiment will be the same."

Maggy swallowed. "In case you're wondering, you're not really selling this."

She reached out for her water glass and was horrified to see her hand was shaking again. She dropped it back to her lap and only frowned when Reza poured her a glass of wine instead and set it before her. Wine, she thought, would not help this situation at all. It would blur everything and complicate it far too much.

And God knew she'd never manage to keep her hands to herself with a glass or two of wine in her.

The fact that notion made her feel something like seasick didn't make it any less true.

"Never fear," Reza said as he sat back in his seat. "You have a secret weapon that will make all of this child's play."

This time her smile came a little more easily. "Do you mean my biting wit? Or maybe you mean my famous charm. Both known as weapons in their way, you're right."

His gray eyes gleamed silver in the candlelight. "I mean me."

CHAPTER FOUR

"YOU," MAGGY SAID, sounding as resoundingly un-impressed as ever, which might have dented Reza's confidence somewhat had he not been, for all intents and purposes, bulletproof. He was the king of the Constantines. He'd learned from his father's mistakes and the collapse and war Reza had narrowly avoided. His confidence was unassailable. "You are my secret weapon."

"No need to fall all over yourself to thank me," Reza said drily. "It is but one of my many royal duties to aid a lost princess in her time of need."

Her captivating eyes narrowed. "Let me guess. You run a royal princess rescue and travel the world, collecting princesses wherever you roam and then holding adoption events on Saturdays."

Reza found himself paying far too much attention to her impertinent mouth, and not only because of the astonishing things that came out of it. He ordered himself to raise his gaze to hers again.

"I have always been good with strays, Magdalena," he told her, his voice low, and he was sure he could see goose bumps prickle over the exposed skin at her neckline. He liked that far more than he should when she was such an unrefined little thing, scrappy and sharp. "It is always about letting them know two things."

"Wait. I know this one." Her gaze flashed with something too dark for simple temper. "Something about how you're a mighty king. And then something else about how, in case anyone missed it, you're a mighty, mighty king."

He had no idea why, instead of igniting his outrage the way it should have done and would have done with anyone else, her arch tone and the matching look on her face made him bite back a wholly unexpected surge of amusement instead. Reza didn't know whether he was baffled by her behavior—or at himself. Both, perhaps.

"One," he said, as if she hadn't spoken, because that was clearly the safer course, "that they are safe at last. And two, that it is far better to have me as an ally than an enemy."

"I bet that goes over really well with the average puppy," Maggy murmured, as disrespectfully as ever. "It must make potty training a breeze."

And it occurred to Reza then, as they sat there on opposite sides of the small table and Maggy's guarded caramel gaze was fixed to his as if she was expecting an attack at any moment, that he was unused to participating in interactions with women when he didn't already know the outcome.

Such things simply never happened, not even back when he'd been at Cambridge and had enjoyed the illusion of slightly more freedom while his father had run the country toward ruin. He'd still had guards who made sure no one ever got too close to him or approached him without permission, especially any women he might have wanted to meet. And even then, he'd been too conscious of the responsibilities that waited for him and his own father's *do as I say, not as I do* expectations of his behavior to risk something that could end up in tabloid photographs and appalling tell-alls.

As a sitting monarch—and the son of a father who had bent the rules because he'd allowed himself to get into a position where he could be blackmailed in the first place—Reza obviously could not date. He could not participate in anything remotely like a date, in fact. In the years before he'd been seriously looking for an appropriate queen, he'd had to find his women a different way entirely, as there could be no chance meetings for a man in his position. No happening upon a bar or whatever sort of place single people congregated. No accidental meetings of the friends of his friends, given that no one appeared in his presence without both permission and a thorough vetting. Reza's advisers presented him with thick dossiers detailing any woman deemed appropriate for his notice. He sifted through them when he was of a mood until he found any who appealed to him. When he did, arrangements would be made to meet privately, usually at dinners like this one or with a careful selection of very old friends who proved indisputably loyal and discreet.

But the women in question, vetted or not, had ample time to decline the invitation to meet with him before they ever set foot in any room where he might appear. Refusals were not common, of course. Still, they happened every now and again. Reza was a powerful and public figure forever bound to his country first. Some women didn't wish to put themselves into that kind of fishbowl, and how could he blame them?

The ones who did, the ones who met him in artfully arranged places like this one far away from the eyes of the world, were always sure things. Give or take a bit of artful flirtation and the appropriate amount of flattery on his side and awe on theirs, if they sat down with him, they were his.

His lost princess, however, was nothing like a sure thing. She had thus far ignored every reference he'd made to the fact they had been betrothed years ago and, beyond that, made no secret of the fact she did not exactly respect him or even note his eminence. These things were remarkable enough. But more than that, Reza found the unusual sensation of being in some suspense about what might happen here made him…restless.

Maggy sat before him as if she wasn't the least bit intimidated by him—still. When she'd clearly discovered that he was exactly who he'd said he was. It pricked at something in him, that her disrespect hadn't eased in any way. The truth was, he'd expected her to have a full personality shift into the sort of overawed obsequiousness that usually marked his interactions with other people. Especially because she was the only living human who had ever insulted him to his face. He'd imagined this woman would be even more determined to smooth things over with him now that she knew his identity.

That she did not appear to care in the least what he thought of her seemed to stroke him, like hot hands all over his body.

Which was not acceptable. At all.

"What exactly do you want to do to me?" she asked, snapping him back to the dinner at hand.

And for a moment Reza was entirely a man. Not a king. Another sensation that was entirely new to him, and threw him into his father's territory. *I am as much a man as I am a king*, his father's voice echoed in his head. It should have appalled him. Yet he was focused much too intently on her lush mouth, not to mention all the things he'd like to do with that mouth—

Enough. This was neither the time nor the place. This wasn't who he was. He'd made certain of it.

But his body was not paying the slightest bit of attention to his cool, rational mind. It wanted her.

He wanted her.

Not as the queen he'd been promised since her birth, though he wanted that, too. But as a man.

Reza had absolutely no idea what to do with that. Of course, it was not his emotions. Not with a woman who still looked like a servant. Though the fact it was something far more earthy didn't exactly thrill him.

"Because I have to tell you," she was saying, utterly unaware of what was happening to him as far as he could discern, and thank God for that, "as amusing as it is to be compared to an entire zoo's worth of rescue animals, I'm going to go out on a limb and say that, probably, I don't want to do it. Whatever it is."

He was relieved—to an unseemly degree—when the doors opened again and his staff swept in, trading out one course for the next with brisk efficiency. He ordered himself under control, and for the first time in a life dedicated to his duty and the necessity of projecting a great calm whether he felt it or not, he wasn't sure he could manage it.

What the hell was happening to him? Was he genetically predisposed to repeat his father's great folly? He would not allow it. He could not.

Reza glanced up when the door did not close behind the waitstaff, to see his own personal aide waiting there. Something pounded in him, hard and triumphant. Because this was a formality. He was sure of it.

"Do you have a result?" he asked his man.

He was aware of the way Maggy stiffened in her seat across from him. And more curious, the fact she didn't turn around to look toward the door. She kept her eyes on the plate before her and her hands in her lap. He was certain that if he looked more closely, she'd have balled them into fists. But he kept his gaze trained on the man at the door instead.

"It is a match, sire," the man said, as Reza had known he would since the moment he'd seen that picture of Maggy ten days ago.

He nodded his thanks and his dismissal at once. His blood seemed to roar through him, making him hard and focused and *needy* in a way he didn't quite understand. He was not a man who *needed. A good king does not need the things a man does*, his mother had always told him. The memory set Reza's teeth on edge. He was a king who had all that he needed, thank you. He'd never felt anything like this in his life.

But he kept his voice cool when he spoke, amazed that it, too, was far more difficult than it should have been.

"Congratulations, Princess." He waited for her to look at him, but she didn't. He studied the elegant line of her neck that no cheap black dress could obscure. There were centuries of good breeding right there in her still form. And she would be his queen. All of him—man and king alike, not that he'd ever found there to be much difference between the two before tonight—exulted. "You are, as expected and now beyond any shadow of doubt, Magdalena of Santa Domini."

Naturally, *this* woman did not swoon. Or carry on in any way. Or even seem to react to the news that must surely have been near enough to magic or a lottery win after so many years of hardship and toil. She took a breath that was slightly deeper than any she'd taken before, that was all. Then she raised her head.

There was no joy there on her lovely face. No gleam of victory or relief. Her caramel gaze was flat. Blank.

Reza found her fascinating. And that was the trouble. He had wanted women before, in appropriately discreet ways. He had enjoyed their company, but mostly that was because every woman he'd ever encountered—especially in private—had dedicated herself to entertaining him until the inevitable day he lost interest. He hardly knew what to make of this, that his lost betrothed was about as enamored of him as she was of the table they sat at, and made no attempt to hide it. And while all his previous mistresses seemed to blur together in his mind, this princess who called herself Maggy and sat there before him with badly colored blond hair and a dress that could most charitably be called beneath her station…was not blurry at all. If anything, she was the only thing in sharp, intense focus.

He only just repressed the urge to shake his head, as if to clear it.

"What if there's been a mistake?" she asked.

"There is no room for error," he told her. He found it was preferable to discuss concrete facts than it was to interrogate himself about the strange things happening inside of him tonight. "For various security reasons, samples of many royal families' blood are taken and stored. One never knows the circumstances under which one's identity or paternity might be called into question. A sample of yours was given to my family when our betrothal contracts were executed. Your blood tonight has matched it." He studied her proud, intent face. "There is no mistake."

He watched, drawn to her in a way he chose not to analyze just then, as she reached up and rubbed behind her ear with one finger. Touching that birthmark that marked her, the same way he had earlier.

Again, he expected a reaction. And again, he was disappointed.

Maggy only swallowed, as if against a constriction in her throat, but when she spoke her voice was smooth. "What happens now?"

Reza needed to get ahold of himself. If only because it was unacceptable to imagine any scenario in which the king of the Constantines was the *less* composed person in a room. In any room.

"First, you must look the part," he said, forcing himself to concentrate on the practicalities. Not this madness that was sweeping through him, rendering him a stranger to himself. When he had known exactly who he was and all the contours of the life he would lead from the day of his birth, and had never deviated from that knowledge in all his life. Especially when it came to matters of the flesh, after his father's terrible example.

Uncertainty did not suit him. It horrified him, in fact. Deeply.

Maggy's unreadable eyes were fixed on him. "You said I already look like the late queen. Problem solved."

He noticed she did not refer to Queen Serena as her mother, but he tucked that away. "I'm afraid it is not your bone structure that the paparazzi will focus on."

"Oh, wait." Her caramel gaze turned hostile then. But not surprised. "What you're trying not to say is that I don't look like a princess. I probably look like a cheap townie who's had to work her ass off to get anything she has, no matter how crappy it looks to visiting royalty. Because guess what? That's who I am."

Reza did not quite sigh. "I cannot imagine any reason the phrase *cheap townie* would exit my lips," he told her. He eyed her mutinous expression. "And certainly not as a description of the woman I am contracted to marry."

"I don't know why not," she retorted. Once again sliding right past their betrothal. Reza found that fascinating, too. What he didn't know was if that was because he was interested in what she tried to ignore—or if his ego was a bit stung by the continuing proof that this woman was the only one alive who, apparently, wasn't transported into a froth of joy at the idea of marrying him. He had the lowering suspicion it was the latter, especially as Maggy kept going, her voice hard. "You weren't quite this shy or retiring back in the coffee shop. Hit me with it. I can take it." She lifted her hands, palms up, but didn't shift her gaze from his. "Tell me all the ways I'm defective. I dare you."

Reza was not used to direct challenges. Much less outright dares. And he was certainly not used to such displays from those who ought to have found his very presence nothing short of miraculous. Worth gratitude, at the very least—but he shoved that aside. That was most definitely his ego talking. The inbred arrogance he'd been born with. He was self-aware enough to recognize he had both in abundance. What he didn't recognize—and did not care for one bit— was this uncontrolled, dark thing he couldn't identify as it swelled in him. It was as if with her, he truly was nothing but a man.

From one breath to the next, he couldn't decide if that was unforgivable or intriguing.

Nonetheless, he took that dare.

"That false color in your hair does not suit you," he told her, keeping his tone even, because he was a king, not a common lout. He did not attack those weaker than him, or in need of his aid. And no matter the mouth on her, his lost princess was very much both. He needed to keep his heavier artillery to himself. "And only partly because it is inexpertly applied. But the rest is a cosmetic matter, easily handled. A question of more appropriate clothing. Garments made to flatter your particular figure rather than off some bargain rack somewhere. Some tutoring in deportment, so you might comport yourself in a manner more in line with your heritage. Perhaps even some time in a spa to tend to your general air of exhausted desperation."

"It must be some spa," Maggy replied darkly, "to combat twenty years of poverty and loneliness. Will a massage do the trick, do you think? Or will I need something a little more theatrical to get the stink out, like some of those hot stones?"

"You asked me to tell you these things and I thought you could take it. Did you not say so?"

"This is me taking it. I didn't promise I'd be mute." She pressed her lips together for a moment. "Anyway, I don't care about cosmetic things. This might be hard for you to comprehend, but for some people, primping is pretty far down the list."

"That is all very well for a coffee shop drone in the middle of nowhere." He lifted his shoulder, then dropped it. "But we are no longer speaking of that woman. We are speaking of a princess who will return from the dead and find herself in the center of intense public scrutiny."

"You mean me. Not a random, theoretical princess. Me." Maggy shook her head. "And let me tell you something about me, since you're so interested. You can't pretend the last twenty years didn't happen, no matter what a blood test says. *I* certainly can't."

"Do you wish to be ridiculed?" he asked her quietly. "Do you imagine you will enjoy snide tabloid articles about your inability to attend to your own grooming? You didn't care for it when I called you a wild animal. Will you like it when the tabloids screech that you are a feral creature more deserving of a wilderness habitat than a palace?"

She looked as if he'd thrust his fork into her jugular, and he didn't much care for the sensation.

"These are realities you must consider now. Who you are is essentially meaningless. It is who you let them see that matters." He waved a hand at her dress, obviously mass-produced, which hugged her figure in a way that would have rendered his own ruthlessly correct mother pale with horror. Reza found that the man in him appreciated the close embrace of all that cheap, stretchy black material more than he wished to admit. "You cannot simply throw on any old thing and step out in it."

"This is the only dress I own," she said, her tone a frozen thing. "I apologize if it offends you. Had I known that I'd be having dinner with a mighty king, I might have made a trip to the mall."

He placed it then. She almost sounded as if he'd hurt her feelings. He couldn't imagine how.

"I am not insulting you," he told her, frowning. "I am trying to prepare you for what will come. You will need to plan your appearances very carefully, as you will no longer be a private citizen. You will represent the crown."

"As its ungroomed, trailer trash face in a cheap black dress. The poor crown. What if I tarnish it?"

Something inside of him turned over, surprising him.

"Do you think you are the only one who finds these boundaries and necessities absurd?" he bit out at her, and the fact he was shocked by the flare of his own temper should have kept him from continuing. But it didn't. "Insulting, even? Let me assure you that you are not. But there are things that matter more than your feelings."

"So far," Maggy said softly, "it seems that everything matters more than my feelings."

"You can, of course, be the sort of royal beloved by the tabloids for different reasons," Reza said, his tone grim. "There are any number of blue-blooded tarts who fall in and out of Spanish clubs and make fools of themselves at so-called 'edgy' parties in Berlin. The brightest beaches in the Côte d'Azur have dark and desperate shadows where many an heiress loses her way, usually quite publicly. This is always a path that is open to you, if you wish it. You would hardly be the first princess to choose hard partying over hard work."

"Yes," she said, her words a bare whisper, though her caramel eyes were fixed to his and glittered hard with something much darker—something he felt like an echo deep inside of him, and he didn't like it at all. "My goal in life is to be an international whore. It seems like such an upgrade."

Heat seemed to rise in the air between them, electric and impossible. Reza did not want to imagine this woman as any kind of whore, international or otherwise. Or perhaps the truth was, now that she'd said it, he was having trouble thinking of anything else except how much he'd like to descend into a few depths with her. And what the hell did that make him?

"The choice is yours." He sounded darker than he should have. Grittier. "I, personally, prefer a more respectable approach, but then I have been the ruler of the Constantines since I was twenty-three. There was no time for me to make a name for myself in all the wrong ways."

Maggy folded her hands in her lap and Reza suspected it was to keep them from shaking. And if so, he wanted to know if it was anger or some other emotion that worked in her—like maybe some faint echo of the things he felt inside himself that were causing far too much of a commotion. She sat tall in her seat, and he wondered if she knew how very regal she looked while she did it. Or if it was something innate in her. As if her very bones had been calling out her true identity all this time, if only someone had thought to look in the back of beyond and on the wrong continent.

"But nothing you're telling me is about me, really," she said after one long moment dragged into another. She held his gaze and there was no pretending he didn't still see the challenge in her eyes. In the proud tilt of her chin. It was as novel as it was astounding. "You didn't come all this way with a lab in your back pocket because you were concerned about *me*. This entire thing is all about you."

"I beg your pardon?"

That particular tone of his usually ended conversations and led straight to abject apologies and groveling. Maggy didn't appear to hear it—much less heed it. She looked at him with challenge all over her face and not a single trace of anything like respect.

"You don't care what kind of princess I am. You care what kind of queen I might make you, in the unlikely event I actually ever marry you."

Reza paid no attention to that roaring thing in him that was eating him alive. He focused on her, making no attempt to hide the full force of his intent. His need. His royal will that had so far gone uncontested in every way that mattered.

She might be something different than what he was used to. He might find her far more fascinating than was wise or good. She might seem to speak to a part of him he hadn't known was there and didn't like at all—as it seemed a bit too close to the sort of nonsense that had made his father a weak, sentimental, and ultimately dangerous man behind the mask of the decent enough king he'd been before the end. But that didn't change the fact that he would get what he wanted.

He always did.

"You are Princess Magdalena of Santa Domini," he told her. "It is not your choice whether or not to marry me, I'm afraid. It is your destiny."

Maggy didn't feel like a princess. She felt turned inside out. It stood to reason she didn't feel like anybody's *destiny*, either.

Especially not his. No matter what that blood test had said.

"In my experience," she said in a low voice, somehow keeping that raw, scraped hollow thing inside of her at bay a little longer, "*destiny* is a word people use when they don't have a good reason for doing the thing they want to do, but they want permission to go ahead and do it anyway."

Reza pushed back from the table then, getting to his feet. Maggy didn't know why it surprised her— or maybe that wasn't the right word. It was more that when he moved, she *felt* it. It seemed to wrap tight around her and tug. There was a certain powerful smoothness to him. A different sort of danger. It made her belly fold in on itself and feel something like precarious.

She didn't want to keep sitting there like a target while he was moving around the room, so she got to her feet, too, hardly sparing a glance for the perfectly prepared roast that she hadn't so much as touched.

The king who'd told her she was a princess and, more than that, *his* moved from the seating area near the fire to the windows and stood there. She knew he couldn't really be gazing out at the mountains. It was too dark and she could see her own reflection from farther back in the room. He clasped his hands behind him in a way she found deeply royal even if she'd never given a moment's thought to what that might mean before.

Whatever a king was supposed to be, Reza looked the part. It only called more attention to the fact that she was about as far away from a princess as it was possible to get. She didn't need to consult her phone to understand that a stretchy dress from a low-market chain store was not what most European royals wore.

Not even that endlessly trendy royal from England who was always on the front page of everything.

What she didn't understand was the way her stomach twisted at the thought she'd somehow...let Reza down.

You are pathological, she snapped at herself.

"You were promised to me at your birth," he said after a long moment. Maggy had the distinct impression he'd been watching her through the glass. And she was surprised at the gruffness in his voice. That and how it washed over her, like a caress. Like his hand against her face once more. She tried to blink that away. "Our fathers were, if not friends precisely, fond of each other and, more than that, committed to peace and prosperity in both our kingdoms. Combining our countries in marriage pleased them both—and made a great deal of sense in other ways, as well." Beyond him, the dark valley spread out toward the next set of hills, twinkling with village lights like grounded stars. But somehow, Maggy couldn't quite find them soothing. "I always knew I was to marry you. This meant that any youthful, adolescent shenanigans would affect you directly. I therefore kept such things to a minimum, so as to cause neither your father nor mine any embarrassment. Whatever life I wanted to lead, I always knew that there had to be room in it for you."

Maggy thought of her own adolescence. Empty and often painful. She'd thought of no one but herself because she'd had no one but herself. It wasn't selfishness if it was pure survival, surely. Because no one else had cared if she lived or died.

She had no idea how to reconcile those barren years with what he was telling her. The idea that anyone had ever cared about her, even in the most abstract way, simply didn't make sense.

"You must have hated me." Her voice was low. "I would have hated it if I had to live my life based on some stranger."

Even as she said that, she knew it was a lie. That was true now. But there was a time Maggy would have given anything to think something—*anything*—she did or said or was mattered to another living soul.

Reza shook his head. In the glass, Maggy could see herself and his outline, as if the harsh beauty of his face was too much for mere glass to handle.

"You were mine," he said gruffly, and she told herself she didn't notice the way that seared into her. Like electricity. Like some kind of truth. "And I was under no illusions about the life I was expected to lead. I was bred to rule a country, not cater to my own self-interest. I assumed I would be lucky enough to rule it with a queen raised in a similar fashion, who would want the same things I did."

"What is that, exactly?" she asked, and there was some of that electricity in her voice, making it tighter than it should have been. "Because I wanted a roof over my head. A safe place to sleep. What does a king want from life that he doesn't already have every time he snaps his fingers?"

"My people safe, first and foremost," he told her, with another one of those shrugs that made her long for things she couldn't quite name. It was something about the width of his shoulders, the bold, masculine line of his back. "But beyond that, I want what any man wants, if for different reasons. Peace, prosperity, and heirs."

All this time, the conversation had been abstract. To Maggy, anyway. A princess who was to marry and become a queen to a man who was so indisputably a king. All part and parcel of the silly fairy tale this man kept spinning. He might as well have been talking about dancing candelabras or singing crabs for all the impact royalty was likely have on Maggy's life. Even after the aide had come back with the blood test results, she hadn't actually absorbed it.

Yet somehow, *heirs* was the word that smacked into her. It made her realize that whatever else was happening, Reza wasn't kidding around. About any of this. And that this wasn't a fairy tale. This was happening. To her. Right now.

Heirs.

His heirs.

Her heart was beating much too fast and much too hard. She crossed her arms over her chest and tried to hold herself together. And no matter that the empty place deep inside of her was…changing. Growing.

Shifting. An earthquake from the inside out, and it seemed to throb, low and insistent, in her core.

"I've watched a lot of television shows where people carry on about heirs," Maggy managed to say. "I never thought it was a real thing anyone actually did. Meaning, I've literally never heard anyone use that word to describe their kids."

He turned to look at her then, and that was…not better. His gray gaze was dark. It seemed to punch straight through her.

"I will not be leaving my heirs a few pieces of chipped china and furniture of unknown provenance," Reza said softly, and yet there was somehow even more power in his voice than before. "And one does not generally refer to the princes and princesses of the Constantines as *kids*. Moreover, the Constantines are what I will leave them. The House of Argos has held the throne for centuries."

She swallowed and was sure he could hear it. That was how dry her throat was just then. "I'm not sure I'm following you."

"I suspect you are following me perfectly well," he countered, and there was something different in his gaze then. Something almost lazy.

Maggy ignored the flush that moved over her. In her.

"You came to claim me because you thought I was this princess."

"And behold my prescience. You are."

She frowned at him—or more precisely, at the way that gleam in his gaze made her feel a different kind of itchy. Inside and out.

"You found me," she said quietly. "But now what? You want to whisk me off to some palace and make a queen out of me?"

He inclined his head. "I do."

"And where you come from, it's perfectly reasonable to talk about the heirs you need when you talk about things like marriage. To total strangers."

"Mine is a hereditary monarchy, Princess," Reza said in that same low, stirring way. "As such, I only have two jobs. One is to preserve the kingdom. The second is to pass it down to a child of my blood, as my ancestors have done since time immemorial."

"Why haven't you already married?" She studied him as he stood there, straight and tall and arrogant, making it clear he was subjecting himself to her questions because he chose to do so. Not because he had to. Maggy had no idea how he managed to make that so clear. She only knew that something in her thrilled to it. To him. "You've had twenty years to produce heirs with some other appropriate person."

"None of them were quite so perfect for me as you."

What amazed her, Maggy could admit, was how very much she wanted to believe that was a personal comment. A compliment of some kind. Was that how low she'd sunk? That she'd take anything—even this sheer madness—as evidence she didn't have to be quite as alone as she'd always been?

"And by *perfect*, you mean the blood in my veins."

He inclined his head again, though this time, there was something about his hard, stern mouth that got to her. Her heart kicked at her again. Harder this time.

"The blood in your veins is a factor, yes. As is the fact a marriage with a Santa Domini links our kingdoms in precisely the way our fathers envisioned. They were right about the benefits then. I am no less right about those same benefits now. Had all gone as planned, we would have married the moment you came of age."

There was no reason at all that should wind through her the way it did, more of that electricity and something sweet and melting besides. It shouldn't steal her breath, imagining that other life that had been stolen from her. Absurd wealth, yes, but also—and more important, to her mind—family. And perhaps in that alternate reality Maggy might have married this man the way he seemed to think she would have. Which would likely mean she'd already have his children, something she found both impossible to imagine and all too easy to conjure up.

That Maggy would have so much family she would never have to be alone again, unless she chose it.

But that Maggy had been killed in a car accident twenty years ago. The fact Maggy had actually survived the crash didn't change that. She felt herself shiver slightly. Very, very slightly, and she instantly tried to hide it. Still, she thought he saw it.

"So the only difference between me in this scenario and any other trophy wife is that you live in an actual castle, not just a big, tacky house," she managed to say through that same too-tight throat, but she knew she wasn't fighting him any longer.

When exactly were you fighting him? a cynical little voice asked, deep inside. *When you raced to get to this hotel? At his beck and call?*

"I think you will find Constantine Castle to be something of an upgrade from your present circumstances," Reza said quietly, his gaze intent on her. "And that there will be trophies to go around."

And Maggy wasn't a fool. She'd never had the opportunity to be a fool. She'd grown up too fast and much too hard. Like any woman, especially one with limited means, she'd had no choice but to make a study of men. She knew rich men. She knew they did as they liked and expected those they trampled over to thank them for the privilege.

She could only imagine that a king would be even worse.

There was no such thing as fairy tales. She knew that. She'd lived it.

But it seemed as if Reza was the closest she'd ever come. Maggy could imagine a thousand ways she'd come to regret what she was about to do, but at least that would all be new. She'd done this. Poor, scared, alone. She was tired of *this*.

If he said she was a princess, she'd become a princess. If he wanted a queen, she'd do that, too. Hell, heirs weren't an issue, either—if she ignored the *how* and concentrated on what came after that. A baby or two meant that no matter what happened with this man who watched her as if he was another one of the looming mountains outside and he could wait there forever, she could never be discarded again.

She could have everything she ever wanted. All those dreams she'd learned to despise in herself, thinking them a weakness. All those longings she'd tamped down and hidden away, refusing to give in to their lure in the harsh light of day. She could have all of it and a fairy tale, too.

All she had to do was dare to claim it.

"It sounds wonderful," she said, and she ignored the way her voice cracked. Maggy concentrated on the king before her with the hard rain eyes and the future she wanted, no matter the cost. "I can't wait to see it."

CHAPTER FIVE

WALKING AWAY FROM the only life she'd ever known should have been harder.

That was the thought that kept poking at Maggy. It lodged inside her, growing strange talons and digging into her with every breath. She'd always known who she was, or anyway, how she was defined in the community. The lost girl. The discarded girl. She'd been told who she was a thousand times, by well-meaning counselors and harried teachers and unimpressed employers alike. She'd always known exactly what her life entailed, whether she liked it or not. Surely learning that she was wrong about that, that everyone she'd ever known was wrong about that—about everything—should have been as much of a blow as a gift.

But in reality, it couldn't have been easier.

"We will leave in the morning," Reza told her that first night in his sprawling mountain lodge, a certain anticipation making his gray eyes gleam. Or maybe the anticipation was in her, not in him. She couldn't tell. "Do not worry about your possessions or the details of your life here. My people will handle it."

And Maggy had decided to surrender to this, hadn't she? She wanted the fairy tale, whatever it took. She didn't argue with him. She went and sat back down at the table. Then she thought, *what the hell*, and sampled the roast, assuming her appetite would catch up with her. She even took a sip or two of the wine, which was so different from any wine she'd ever tasted before that she couldn't quite believe both could be called by the same name.

"I don't think I can leave the country," she said at one point, glancing up to find Reza still over by the windows, watching her as if she baffled him. There was something else there, in that endlessly dark and gray gaze of his, but she didn't want to look too closely at that. Or the fact she could feel it like an echo inside of her all the same.

"Why not?" he asked, with a mildness she somehow didn't trust.

Maggy shrugged. "I never got a passport. International travel wasn't really on my list of goals these past few years. I've been more interested in other things. Like a steady job, a safe place to crash. You know."

She knew full well he didn't know. That was why she'd said it.

But of course, Reza was unconcerned with such petty things as reality.

"I took the liberty of having my government issue you a passport marking you as a citizen of the Constantines," he told her. "I trust you will find it sufficient to cross any and all borders."

Maggy had a lot of follow-up questions then. When had he had this passport made? What name was on the passport, for that matter? Why was he so certain and simultaneously unconcerned—about everything? But none of those questions mattered, in the long run. They had nothing to do with her goals here, which were fairy tales and her very own family, the end. She needed to keep her focus trained on the prize.

So she only aimed another smile at him, each one easier and smoother than the last. He returned to the table to join her and she kept right on eating, because the courses his staff kept bringing in were a far cry from the cups of noodles she prepared on her hot plate.

Maggy stuffed herself so full she thought she might burst. And she didn't think she'd mind if she did.

The next morning a fleet of sleek, gleaming black SUVs appeared outside the rickety old house where she'd lived these past few years. Maggy came down to meet them with the very few things she considered necessities in a backpack. In a sweatshirt that said STOWE across the front in a nod to a nearby ski resort, her favorite pair of battered jeans, and the boots that had always made her feel tougher than she really was. Blank-faced guards handed her into the SUV in the center of the little convoy. She climbed in and slid across buttery leather seats so soft she was afraid she'd destroy them somehow simply by touching them with her clumsy commoner denim.

But then she found herself inside an enclosed space with Reza, and that was far more alarming than any potential damage she might do to soft leather.

Her heart took up that low, wild beat again. Her blood surged through her in a way that seemed designed to do damage. She was shocked it didn't. And there was that melting, clenching thing, too, low in her belly, making it hard to sit still.

Reza sat next to her as if the spacious backseat was a throne. He took up too much of the available room—or maybe it was that he seemed to claim all the air. He was wearing what she guessed was the royal version of casual. A button-down shirt that looked softer than the leather beneath her, crisp and white against his olive skin, and it amazed her on some distant level how that made her mouth water. He set down the papers he was scanning to look at her as she settled in the seat beside him.

His gaze was stern as it moved all over her, from her hair in a sloppy ponytail to the scuffed toes of her favorite boots.

Maggy stared back at him, her chin rising of its

own accord, far more defiant than the moment called for. But she was seized with a desperate panic as the moment dragged out, even if she thought she'd rather die than let him see it.

Would he think better of this bizarre plan of his? In the cold light of the too-bright winter morning, would he take one look at her and realize that she could never be anything but the discarded piece of trash she'd always been? That there was nothing the least bit royal about her no matter what a blood test had said?

"Today is the last day you will walk around dressed like this in public," he told her, his voice a very calm, very clear command. "And I can only take it as my personal mission to convince you that it is better you do not dress like this in private, either."

"I'm American," she told him, because she preferred to combat nerves with her mouth whenever possible. "I like jeans."

"You are not American," he countered in that same cool way of his that made her whole body overheat. "You have never been American, despite appearances. You are one hundred percent Santa Dominian."

He rapped his knuckles against the window, making her flinch. But it was only his signal to his driver, she realized a moment later. He was giving his men an order, he wasn't having her thrown back into the life she'd decided to leave behind her.

The relief that washed over her then was so intense she was afraid it might flip over the SUV.

"Santa Domini means nothing to me," she murmured. She could only hope he hadn't seen her reaction, or if he had, she assured herself he wouldn't know what it meant. "It's as much a fairy tale to me as you are."

She shouldn't have said that. If she could have snatched the words back, she would have. Maggy glared down at her ratty old orange backpack and tried to pretend she couldn't feel his assessing gaze light up the side of her face, like an open flame.

But the truth was, she felt it everywhere. She felt *him* everywhere.

"I have no objection to jeans, per se," he said as the SUV started down the road, surprising her. "There is a time and place for them, of course. These are not the eighteen hundreds. What I object to is cheap fabric and unflattering, mass-produced cuts that do not flatter your form in any way."

She forgot she was trying to avoid looking at him and shifted to frown at him then. "But—"

Reza only held up a hand, in that way of his, as if he was holding an invisible scepter. "When I have outfitted you in a manner consistent with your actual station in life, if you truly wish to spend your time in the clothes you've brought with you, then we will revisit this conversation."

He didn't wait for her response. He returned to

his papers without sparing Maggy another glance. And it took her longer than it should have to really notice that he'd ended the conversation entirely on his terms, not on hers.

I think you can probably get used to that, she told herself as Deanville slid past her window. *That seems very king-like behavior.*

But the truth was, she couldn't bring herself to care about that as much as she should have. She was too focused on all the things she *wasn't* feeling about leaving the only home she'd ever known. Maggy knew every street, every hill, every tree on the way out of town. She'd been found on Route 132 in Strafford, which was how she'd gotten her surname, and she'd spent the longest stretch of time in a foster home in Deanville. These things—these places—should have left their marks on her. They must have. Yet she felt far more marked, and indelibly, by the man who sat beside her.

And when the convoy delivered them straight out onto the tarmac of a private airfield, not far from a sleek jet embossed with a very intricate and glossy coat of arms, Maggy stopped worrying about the separation anxiety she definitely wasn't feeling about leaving her old existence. Instead, she started panicking slightly about the fact she'd never been on a plane in her life.

"Are you well?" Reza asked as they stood on the tarmac, the sun making the cold bite of the winter air seem less harsh than it was. "You've gone unusually quiet."

"You don't know me well enough to know what's usual or unusual," Maggy pointed out.

His hard mouth almost quirked. "Answer the question, please."

She took her time looking at him. At his ruthless, forbidding face that seemed to fill a thirst in her she hadn't known she had. Maggy had no idea what that meant. She wasn't sure she wanted to know. But she wasn't used to anyone paying such close attention to her.

Something she really didn't want to share with him.

"I'm terrific," she told him. "Never been better, in fact."

She expected him to throw something back at her, or glare in his kingly way. Reza did neither. His expression was too fierce and his mouth was that stern, unsmiling line. But then her breath caught in her throat, because he reached out and smoothed his hand over the length of her ponytail, not quite tugging it, and for a moment it was as if they were the only two people in all the world.

It made her heart flip over.

She was very much afraid that he could hear it.

One mad beat of her heart. Then another. And then Reza dropped his hand and touched her gently at the small of her back, indicating she should walk ahead of him toward the jet while his aides converged around him.

And it took her the whole way up the metal stairs and into the plane, waved in by smiling flight attendants, to catch her breath and get the wild drumming of her pulse under control.

Once on board, she had other things to think about, like the fact there was gold everywhere. Dark, gleaming wood. Thick, soft rugs at her feet. Especially when she was shown past what looked like a luxurious hotel living room into a fully outfitted bedroom suite. On a *plane*.

"Please don't hesitate to ring if you need anything, Your Highness," the flight attendant who'd escorted her said with a smile. "Anything at all."

And it wasn't until the uniformed man walked away that Maggy realized what had happened. That when the man had said *Your Highness*, he'd meant Maggy.

She had to close the door of her suite and sit on the wide, soft bed for a little while then. Until she found her breath again and got her head to stop spinning.

This is what you wanted, she told herself, trying to breathe in and out without hyperventilating. She ran her palms up and down her thighs, the feel of her same old jeans somehow even more disturbing. As if they could somehow snap her back to Deanville if she wasn't careful. Maggy promised herself she'd burn them at the first opportunity.

This is who you are now, she chanted to herself. *You need to figure out how to deal with it.*

But it took her a long while to pull herself together.

The flight was long and smooth. It was also one of the most pleasant experiences of Maggy's life. Every time she stepped outside her suite, there was a different selection of tempting foods laid out in the living room area. Sometimes Reza was out there on one of the sofas, but other times he was off in one of the other rooms in the jet. There was a guarded office, a conference room, bedrooms. An area featuring armchairs and tables where more guards sat, mixed in with a set of always busy-looking people that Maggy assumed were the king's top aides. Maybe his cabinet. None of them looked up when she walked past, stretching her legs, and yet she was sure she could feel their eyes on her back.

And when they finally landed, it was dark.

"Is this your kingdom?" she asked Reza when he escorted her off the plane. There was a strange, heavy salt scent to the air as they crossed another, smaller tarmac and climbed into one more waiting SUV. All the lights had halos around them and her head seemed to spin. She felt hollow straight through.

"Not quite," he replied, and she told herself it was her odd exhaustion that was making him sound like that. As deep and as dark as the night around them. "This island has been in my family for a very long time. It was a gift from an ancient Venetian doge for services rendered, or so the story goes. It will serve as a decent way station, I think."

Maggy felt muddled and thick from the long flight. She wanted to ask him what he meant by calling this a way station. She wanted to ask him if he'd take her to see the sea for the first time. It took her another beat to realize that the ocean itself was that scent in the air, like a rough magic threaded through the night. But she couldn't seem to make her body respond to any of the half-cooked thoughts whirling around and around in her head. She slumped against yet another soft leather seat back and didn't know where the SUV ended and the strange feelings inside of her began. And meanwhile, the world outside the window was nothing but dark in all directions. No towns, no cities. No lights. As if he'd carried her off the side of the world.

She didn't realize she'd fallen asleep until there were suddenly too many lights and a new sort of commotion woke her.

Maggy pushed herself to sitting position and it took her much too long to recognize that she'd fallen asleep with her head on Reza's wide shoulder. The scent in her nose now wasn't the sea. It was him. Faintly spiced, warm male. A far deeper and more treacherous magic and this one seemed to pool deep inside of her, making her core tighten, then ache. Her breath left her in a rush and her eyes flew to his—

To find him watching her in that way of his, his

gray eyes dark. And that all too knowing silvery gleam in his gaze. As if he could tell that just then— one hand at his lean, hard side and the other on his muscled arm, the impression of his shoulder against her cheek—she wasn't thinking of him as a king at all.

Something rolled over her, intense and searing. She was suddenly aware of how terribly, inescapably *hot* she was. So hot she was surprised she wasn't glowing like those lights, with her own bright halo marking her as out of her depth and overheated as she felt.

"We have arrived at the villa," he told her quietly. It occurred to her to wonder how long he'd sat there, letting her sleep on him, before waking her. The idea that it might have been more than the moment or two it took to park wound tight inside of her, lit white-hot and bright. "Can you walk or shall I carry you?"

She couldn't tell if he was kidding. Not that he struck her as much of a kidder. The air between them seemed…taut. Charged. Maggy let go of him entirely and threw herself back across the seats, then told herself she didn't care if he could see her panic. As long as there was space between them. As long as she stopped touching him.

It made that unsmiling mouth of his soften slightly.

"I can walk," she said. Too quickly.

Her voice gave away too much. She could hear it.

And more, she could see the way his eyes went dark, the gleam in them very silver and very, very male. It connected hard to something she hadn't known was there inside of her, making her core shiver, then melt.

Over and over again.

"As you wish, Princess," Reza murmured, laughter in his voice that she could see nowhere on his harsh face. "Welcome to the island."

And then he climbed out of the SUV, leaving her to sit there with only her too-loud breath for company. Wondering what might have happened if she'd said something else. If she hadn't let go.

If she'd moved toward him rather than away.

Reza stood out on the wide stone balcony that surrounded the master suite in the villa, paying no attention whatsoever to the frigid winter temperature as he let the crisp sea air wash all over him.

He needed to wash himself clean of this affliction.

Of this abominable *need* that was eating him alive from the inside out.

He didn't understand what was happening to him. Why the slightest, most innocuous touch from Maggy all but wrecked him. How was she managing it? How had she located the chinks in his armor when he'd had no idea it was armor in the first place? He'd thought this was simply who he was—unassailable in all ways—until now.

Was he more his father's son than he had ever imagined? Was it possible?

The cold night beat at him, but he didn't move inside.

This island had always been his family's retreat. Back when Reza was a boy, this was where his parents took him at least once a year so that the royal family could have some time away from the pressures of court and the endless scrutiny of the public. When he was older, he'd realized it was where his parents came to hash out their differences—meaning, his father's betrayals—in a place his father couldn't retreat. The one place his father's mistress wasn't available at a moment's notice, allowing his mother the chance to pretend the other woman didn't exist. Fittingly, this was where they'd taught him that he was never, ever to behave as if he was flesh and blood and a mortal like all the rest. Like them.

This was where he'd learned that there was no room in the king for any hint of the man.

It does not matter what you say, Reza, but what you do, his mother had told him again and again, that harsh look in her gaze not for him, he understood in retrospect, but aimed at him all the same. *Your subjects want to follow a king they can admire and support, not a flawed, weak little man whose clay feet trip him up whenever he tries to stand.*

His mother had been a remote parent and a distant queen. She'd believed her place was behind the king, silent and beautiful and ever supportive, and no matter the whispers about her husband's long-term dalliance or where his obsession with that woman had led him as the leader of a country. As far as Reza knew, she had never indicated in any kind of public setting that she even knew the other woman existed. *The people are interested in the king, never his consort*, she would tell her aides reprovingly when they'd broach the possibility of an interview or an article, perhaps talking about both of her husband's women. And then she'd proved that her devotion outstripped her rival's beyond a shadow of a doubt when she'd followed the king into the hereafter within three years of the death she'd known full well was no random heart attack. She had been a beacon of *correctness* unto the grave, and all the better if she'd been able to use it as a weapon. That was his mother. Ferocious in her pain unto the end.

Reza had not brought Maggy, his feral princess, here by accident.

But even now, even as he stood out in the cold and tried to lecture himself back into the closed-off, hermetically sealed state he had long preferred, Reza couldn't quite manage it. He couldn't stop thinking about Maggy.

The fact he was thinking of her as *Maggy* at all, instead of the more sophisticated, regal, and thus far more appropriate *Magdalena*, was part of the problem.

She'd shuffled out of her house dressed like a Halloween costume version of a young American woman, all attitude and that stubborn chin. But then, her wide caramel eyes had told him she was far more anxious than she appeared. She'd looked more vulnerable in that harsh morning light. Less hardened by the life she'd led than she had the night before.

He hadn't known how to identify the feeling that had worked in him then. He hadn't the slightest idea what it was. It had taken him the entire ride to the airport, reading and rereading the same three sentences on the same damned document, to understand what it was.

Helpless.

He was Reza Argos. He was the king of the Constantines. He was not and never had been and never would be anything like *helpless*. The very idea was laughable.

But then he'd proved that wasn't true at all when he'd touched her again, running his hand over that brash, blond hair that was nonetheless silky and smooth against his palm. He'd stood too close to her out on that tarmac. She'd smelled vaguely of vanilla and coconut, and even that had slammed through him like a caress against the hardest part of him. And that same feeling had washed through him again.

He couldn't help himself. He couldn't stop.

He had no idea what the hell he was doing or when

he'd become a slave to his feelings like his father. He only knew he couldn't allow it.

Reza was no untouched, untried boy. Yet here he stood on the other side of the planet, the cold wind from the Adriatic Sea pummeling him, and all he could think about was the way she'd looked at him back on a tarmac in the middle of nowhere in Vermont. What was happening to him?

Why was he *letting* this happen to him, and with the most unlikely creature imaginable? Did he care so little for his own pride—the promises he'd made himself that he would never, ever succumb to weakness like his father?

And that was before she'd fallen asleep on his shoulder.

It was a ten-minute drive from the airfield on the southern tip of the island to the magnificent villa that stood at its highest point, commanding views over the sea in all directions. And Reza had sat there perfectly still, unwilling to dislodge the soft weight of her.

Unwilling or unable. He couldn't decide which. He'd been lost somewhere in the heat of her body against his. The faint press of her against him. The way her head seemed crafted especially to fit right there on his shoulder—

"Sire."

His aide's voice came from behind him, snapping him out of the memory of her body next to his, and

Reza didn't turn. He worried at what might be on his face. What he might reveal without realizing it. What might very well be shining off of him like a beacon, betraying every last thing he'd become. Showing that he'd turned into the very thing he hated.

"Is our guest settled?" he asked. He didn't like the effort it took to sound as calm as he usually did.

"Yes, sire. In the queen's suite, as you wished." His aide cleared his throat. "And everything is arranged for the morning, in accordance with your orders."

Reza turned then, nodding his acknowledgment and then following his aide back into the villa. He closed the doors against the winter chill, then stood in the great expanse of the bedroom that he'd once believed was the size of the world. He'd been allowed in here so rarely as a child. It had been his father's private retreat. He'd hidden away in here from the family he'd supposedly come to the island to spend time with in the first place.

As a small boy, Reza had wanted nothing more than to come in here. Now he viewed it as a monument to a past he had best start paying better attention to before he repeated it.

He hardly noticed when his aide left him to his thoughts.

The fact that he'd located the lost Santa Domini princess should have made him happier. He understood this. He'd not only found her, he'd rescued her from a life that was so far beneath her it astounded him. And more, he'd brought her here to this island to teach her not only how to step back into the life she'd been stolen from, but how to operate as his queen.

After all this time, he'd found his queen. The girl he'd been betrothed to when he was all of ten years old. The woman who represented a whole future he'd lost when that car had crashed in Montenegro when he was eighteen.

He'd mourned her—and the loss of the life they'd been meant to build together—for longer than he cared to admit.

But the trouble was, he wanted her. *Want* had never entered into it before, because it was irrelevant. Because he was not his damned father. His kingdom was what mattered. The promises their families had made and the contracts they'd signed were all that had mattered. He'd come of age expecting a queen who would take after his own mother and fade into the background, perfectly pedigreed and unquestionably correct, once she'd done her duty and provided him with an heir.

The trouble with Maggy was that all he could think about was taking her to his bed, and duty had nothing to do with it.

Which meant that for the first time in as long as he could remember, he wasn't doing his.

"What if I'm not a good king?" he'd dared to ask his parents on one of their visits here in a mild autumn. He'd still been so young. He hadn't understood the fierce chill between his mother and father as they'd all walked together. It was all he'd known. They'd strolled down the beach while sweet winds blew in from Venice to the west and off the Gulf of Trieste to the north.

"You will be," his father had told him, with that regal certainty in his deep voice that had straightened Reza's spine. His father had still been so much taller than Reza then, and Reza had been more than a little in awe of him. "Argos men have held the kingdom forever. You will do the same."

He had smiled when he'd looked down at Reza then, an unusual show of the emotion he usually saved for his extramarital relationship, or so the pictures Reza had been forced to destroy after his death suggested.

The queen had not smiled. Her cold eyes had seemed to burn. "You will have no choice."

Reza had never forgotten that.

Because having no choice but to put the kingdom first meant everything else fell into line behind it. Life was simple, in its way, and his father's terrible example had helped make it so. Reza was not burdened with the personal travails that took down so many other men in his position. He had no vices, because they would harm him and thus the kingdom. He had never felt trapped by the security details forever surrounding him and cutting him off from the rest of the world, he'd felt safe. No one touched him. No one had influence over him. He belonged only to his people and the two alpine valleys that had been there in his blood at birth.

And he was at an extreme disadvantage tonight because of it, as he stood in the middle of his bedroom floor, lost in unhelpful images of his future queen. One after the next, as if he had no control at all.

Because the startling truth was that he didn't have the slightest idea what to do with temptation. It had never been a factor.

Reza only knew he had to keep himself from surrendering to this—to her—whatever the cost.

CHAPTER SIX

REZA HADN'T BEEN KIDDING when he'd mentioned a spa, Maggy discovered the next morning.

She'd woken up after a strange night packed tight with odd dreams to find herself in a luxurious, sprawling ancient villa that somehow fused marvelous old Italian touches with surprisingly modern updates, from a perfect bathroom suite to its heated floors. More accurately, she'd been woken up by a cheerful attendant, who'd hurried her out of bed and into a soft robe, pressed an exquisitely made latte into her hands, and then led her through the achingly beautiful villa while she was still sipping at it.

Maggy was far too bleary-eyed to object. She had the hectic impression of graceful rooms filled with dancing morning light, and then she was being led through a warm, glassed-in area where a pretty pool gleamed bright blue in the sun. The attendant led her to the far side of the circular pool, then into an already hot sauna.

"Should you need anything at all, Your Highness, you need only press this button," the attendant told her, collecting Maggy's empty latte mug as she left and closed the heavy door behind her.

Maggy wasn't any more used to hearing herself called that. *Your Highness.* She had to bite back an involuntary giggle. But then again, what part of any of this was she used to? She knew what a sauna was, but she'd never been in one before. She blinked as she looked around the wooden room. It seemed like an outward manifestation of how she felt already—hot and airless and finding it harder to breathe by the second.

But if this was what royals did, then by God, she would do it. She would do anything. *You* are *royal,* she reminded herself. *Your blood proves it.* She sat on the warm wooden slats as soothing new age music piped in, and wondered if maybe she was still sleeping. If maybe she'd wake up to find herself back in her narrow bed in her tiny room back in Vermont, late for work as usual. She reached down and pinched herself, viciously. On her thigh, then on her belly, but nothing happened. It hurt and it left her with two dull red marks, but that was it. She stayed put in this hot, cedar cell. Sweating wildly.

Even so, she couldn't discount the high possibility that this was a dream anyway. She'd had dreams like this before, in shocking, tactile detail. The difference was, Maggy intended to enjoy every minute no matter what. She was resolved. She tipped her head back, figured out how to breathe long and slow when the air felt nearly solid around her, and she let the deep heat soak into her.

When the lights and heat inside the sauna turned themselves off sometime later, she emerged, sleepy-eyed and wrapped in her robe again, to find that a personal spa had been assembled for her in the great, glassed-in space on the warm stones to the side of the pool. Attendants flocked around her, buffing and waxing whatever parts of her they could reach. She was manicured and pedicured. Her brows were shaped and her hair was set with color and then cut without a single word from her. She was served a steady stream of plates filled with colorful, aston-ishingly good food every time she made any kind of eye contact with anyone. She was massaged from head to toe and rubbed down with creams and rinses and who even knew what else, until she felt as if she'd been pummeled into the shape of an entirely new woman.

And when it was all done, her attendants wrapped her in a fluffy towel that could have enveloped a fam-ily of four and then led her back through the villa.

She'd been too dead on her feet the night before and much too bleary this morning as she'd been hus-tled down to the sauna area to really look around. But after a day of more pampering than she'd had in her whole life, she found she could hardly keep herself from happily soaking in the place as she followed the smiling women surrounding her.

Reza had called this *the villa*. But to Maggy, it was a palace. Polished marble stretching in all directions. Rooms filled with precious things beyond description. Couches that looked like works of art all their own, set on rugs that likely were. Gleaming pieces of desperately fancy furniture that were nicer than her entire previous life.

Everywhere she looked there were arches and windows, allowing her to see that the sea was *just there*. It was capped with white and surging deep blue and mighty in all directions, visible from every angle. Every room showed her a new view of the water, making it seem as if the villa itself was floating on the waves. Inside, the ceilings were high and set with intricate panels that she was sure probably had some fancy name she'd never learned. There was art on every wall, and Maggy didn't have to know anything about it to know what she was looking at was priceless. One or two paintings she even thought she might recognize, which she was aware meant they had to be so ridiculously famous someone who'd never looked at a single piece of art in a museum or anywhere else would know them at a glance.

She was in such a completely different world it made her head spin.

This is definitely a dream, that cynical voice inside warned her. *I wouldn't get too comfortable if I were you.*

But she wanted to be comfortable here, and no matter if she woke up tomorrow in her tiny room in Vermont. She wanted to be the princess Reza thought she was, with a family and a history at last. So she did nothing but follow her attendants back through the meandering wing that led to the set of rooms she'd been delivered to the night before. She ignored that voice deep inside. If this wasn't going to last, she wanted to enjoy every last bit of it. The smooth stone floors. The beautiful colors of everything she saw, from old-looking tables to tapestries on the ancient walls, to fresh flowers in every vase on almost every surface though it was still winter outside.

She walked through her private sitting room with its fireplace, cozy sofas, and shelves full of heavy-looking books arranged amid small statues. There were windows that doubled as doors leading out toward the sea, and it made her heart feel light that she could see so far. There was a smudge on the horizon that she was pretty sure was Italy. Or possibly Croatia. And that was according to the map on the sleek, very European smartphone an aide had handed her at some point earlier today.

"For your convenience, Your Highness," the man had murmured.

The phone had exactly one number programmed

into it under the name *Reza Constantines*. Maggy had stared at it. But she hadn't dialed it.

She followed her little entourage into the vast, sprawling bedroom, set with delicate furniture that struck her as feminine and very thick rugs tossed across the stone floor. She'd crashed across the wide, four-poster bed last night in an utter daze as much from the flight as from her nap *on Reza*, and then she'd stared up at the magenta canopy until she'd drifted off approximately four seconds later. But now the bed was made up again as if for a magazine shoot and there were clothes laid out across its foot.

"His Majesty wishes you to meet him in his private salon," one of the attendants told her. "At your earliest convenience."

"I assume that means at *his* earliest convenience," Maggy murmured. She'd meant to sound dry, but she was far too relaxed. It came out much softer than it should have.

The women around her laughed, and that was its own head trip. Maggy was prickly, everybody said so. She couldn't remember the last time a group of people had laughed around her, unless it was *at* her.

"He is the king," one of the women said quietly. "We all serve at his pleasure."

And Maggy felt as if she ought to object to that, on principle if nothing else, but somehow she couldn't quite bring herself to do it. *Later*, she told herself.

You can worry about the king's pleasure *later—or maybe you'll just wake up.*

The women surrounded her again, and after a day of it she let them without another thought. She sat on the vanity stool and realized after a few moments that they were deliberately keeping her from looking in the mirror. She didn't fight it. This was her dream and she was going to eke every drop of this princess routine out of it before she was drop-kicked back to the real world.

Because there was always the chance that wanting this to be real would make it so.

One woman carefully made up her face while another blew out her hair. It took them some time. When they were done, they handed her a pile of soft, impossibly silky things it took her long, confused moments to realize were a bra and panties. Just of a far higher quality than the ones she'd bought herself in cotton value packs.

Even her feet looked like someone else's, she thought as she stepped into the deliriously silky panties behind the towel two attendants held up for her once she shed her robe. Tipped in a rich red now, buffed and sanded smooth and soft, they weren't *her* feet. *Her* feet were usually hard across the heels and aching. The panties fit perfectly, as did the matching bra, and she told herself she wasn't thinking about who could possibly have estimated her measurements so well.

She kept telling herself that even as that same, familiar heat that was all about Reza and his hard, stern mouth rolled over her, then pooled deep in her belly again.

But there was no time for blushing. Her attendants hurried her into the dress that waited for her at the foot of her bed, a dove-gray thing that didn't look very interesting when they held it up, but felt like a whisper once they pulled it over her head. The shoes they slipped on her feet were the same, so high she expected them to pinch and hurt, but instead she felt as if she was wearing bedroom slippers once she stood in them.

It explained a great deal about the things she'd seen famous people wear in magazines. Who could possibly have imagined all those crazy, acrobatic clothes were *comfortable*? No wonder Reza had been so dismissive about her clothes. It all made a lot more sense now.

She felt them fasten something around her neck, cool and slippery against her skin. Someone slid a ring onto her index finger, and then they were bustling her back out of the room. She could see that the sun was setting outside the windows, sinking in an orange blaze toward the sea, but she was dazzled by the lights inside the villa, too. They were everywhere, buttery and bright, making the hallway seem as if it was merry of its own accord.

Or maybe that was just her.

Her attendants hurried her down the hall, and it took her longer than it should have to make the obvious connection that her suite was only the next door down from Reza's—it was just that the rooms in the villa were very large and the hallway connecting them quite long. And in fact, the door in the far wall of her bedchamber that hadn't opened when she'd tried it last night must lead directly into his rooms—a notion that made every nerve ending in her body shiver to instant awareness.

But there was no time to process any of it, because she was being led directly into the king's dazzling suite. His private salon was the size of a hotel ballroom, she thought wildly, looking all around her. The light here was as bright and glorious as the rest of the villa. It bounced off of all the inlaid gold in the different seating areas arranged in little clusters around the big room—here an elegant couch, there an impossibly graceful quartet of chairs. Even the walls themselves were lined with gold, interspersed with a deep crimson. It looked exactly the way Maggy would have imagined a king's room should look, had she ever had cause to think about such things.

And in the center of all that regal brightness stood Reza, in yet another perfectly crafted dark suit that made him look like a storm of a man, his gray eyes fixed to her as if this was the first time he'd ever seen her.

As if, she thought wildly, he'd been waiting his whole life to see her.

Maggy felt that gaze of his like a shudder, a wicked, rolling thing down deep inside of her. A new, dangerous heat bloomed there, then spread, washing over her limbs and making her pulse go liquid.

She was vaguely aware that the attendants left them. She didn't dare move—or she couldn't. And Reza only stood there for what seemed to her to be a long, long time, that stern gaze on her in a way that made her feel as if all the dizzy light in the room was trapped inside of her. A part of her.

She was certain he could see it. That he knew.

"I don't know what they did," she heard herself tell him. She had no idea what she was saying. How could she tell when she didn't sound anything like herself? "They wouldn't let me look."

He said nothing. He merely held out his hand.

Maggy didn't know why she didn't so much as hesitate.

The dream, she told herself, though her dreams had never been *quite* this vivid. *This is all part of the dream.*

The fairy-tale dream she hadn't allowed herself to truly indulge in for years.

She moved across the floor and took the hand he offered her, and only then—when a different blaze of sheer fire poured into her and made her heart kick at her—did she think to question why she'd thrown herself into it like that. Into him. Only then, when it was too late.

But Reza only led her over to a huge mirror left propped up against the wall in the farthest corner of the great room, looking as if it had stood exactly like that for centuries. It likely had. It, too, was edged in a heavy gold frame, as solid and certain as the king himself.

He positioned her in front of the glass and stood behind her. Much too close to her. One hand holding hers and the other a faint pressure at her waist. More of that delirious fire raced through her at the contact, making her legs feel weak. Maggy knew she should push herself away from him. Get his hands off of her, for a start. She knew she should do *something*.

But she couldn't seem to do anything but stare.

"Look at you," Reza murmured, his voice a rough velvet much too close to her ear and the birthmark he'd known was there from the start. "They did exactly as I asked. They made you who you are. Magdalena Santa Domini."

The woman in the huge, gold mirror was...not Maggy. Or if she was, it was a version of herself that Maggy could hardly get her head around. A dream version she never would have dared imagine on her own. Never.

She knew it was her and yet...it couldn't possibly be her.

A princess, a small voice inside her whispered, with something like awe. *You look like a princess.*

They'd dyed her hair back to her natural color, a dark and lustrous chestnut, and they'd swept it back from her face. Still, the light picked up deep golds and russets that seemed to make her eyes glow. And her eyebrows looked elegant, in place of her usual unremarkable brows. Her whole face was smooth and she thought she looked different, and not only because of the subtle makeup they'd put on her. It took her a moment to realize she looked rested. Or not exhausted, anyway.

She'd never seen her own face so bright before.

The dress looked like something out of one of those glossy magazines she'd always pretended to loathe. The gray color was soft and interesting at once, making Maggy's pale skin seem to glow. It was a modest dress, she supposed, but it didn't seem that way. There was something about *how* it fell from a sophisticated neckline all the way to her knees, with only a slight indentation just beneath her breasts, that suggested a kind of restrained and high-class sex appeal without actually showing anything. The shoes did much the same thing, somehow managing to look elegant in a way Maggy didn't know shoes could. There was a gleaming diamond necklace around her neck and a chunky ring on her index finger featuring a collection of precious gems in a variety of colors, all of which caught the light and sparkled.

But more than all that, *she* looked like someone else. Completely different from the Maggy she'd seen in her own mirror yesterday morning before she'd headed out to meet Reza's convoy. If she hadn't known the reflection she was looking at was hers, she'd have easily and happily believed that it was some long-lost princess. And she hardly dared think it, but she really did look like that picture of the queen he'd shown her.

The queen. *Her mother.*

But she didn't want to think about that yet. Not yet. She took a breath and realized in the next instant that Reza was still holding her fingers in his as he stood behind her, his other hand at her waist. And suddenly she could think of nothing else. Except the tempting notion that if she leaned back the tiniest bit she could nestle herself directly against the wall of his chest.

She would never, ever know how she managed to keep herself from doing it.

"This is how you look after one day," Reza told her, his voice near her ear making her shiver. He was the one who stepped away then, something she couldn't read making his eyes silver. She fought to repress yet another shiver as she watched him in the mirror. "We will stay here several weeks. By the end of this time, I expect you will be able to acquit yourself quite well in the glare of whatever spotlight you might encounter."

"Yes," she said, because she had to say something. And she couldn't let herself say any of those things that clawed at her from that raw place, deep inside. She didn't want to think them. She wanted this. She wanted every last part of this. "I'm sure I will."

But even after he turned and headed across the room, Maggy stayed where she was before that great, tipped glass, staring at herself. Because she wasn't herself anymore.

She was the fairy-tale princess he'd made her into, just as he'd said he would, in the course of a single day.

And Maggy had absolutely no desire to ever wake up.

It was worse now she looked the part.

And much, much worse that he'd let himself hold her like that.

Reza told himself this mad obsession was beneath him. That he was in no position to lose himself in a woman like his father had done before him, particularly not this one. If she was to be his queen—and she was, of course, as their fathers had planned so many years ago—then the formalities needed to be observed above all else. The only thing he could think of that was worse than losing his head over an inappropriate mistress was doing the same thing over the woman who would have to bear his children. Where would it end? What destruction would he wreak? He couldn't imagine it. Or allow it.

He spent his days tending to matters of the crown from his office in the villa, surrounding himself with his advisers and running his country from afar. And if he insisted on an investigation into that long-ago accident and the following of twenty-year-old leads to figure out how a Santa Dominian child in a car accident in Montenegro had made it across the Atlantic Ocean to the United States, so be it. The Princess Magdalena was to be his queen. What had happened to her would be public record and, more than that, incorporated into the lore of the monarchy itself.

He filled her days with the very serious business of turning an abandoned American foster child into one of Europe's most celebrated royals.

He had her fitted for an entire new wardrobe that suited her position. He had Milanese courtiers fly in with one of a kind pieces for her to try on and choose between as she pleased, with the help and advice of his personal tailors. He flew in special jewelers from Paris to outfit her appropriately, so she might have a few pieces to wear until she regained her access to the Santa Dominian crown jewels, to say nothing of the Constantinian collection she would be expected to wear after their wedding.

And while all the outward trappings that would cement her as his betrothed in all the right ways were being attended to by the most fashionable people in the world, he brought in diction coaches to soften and shape her language. He couldn't teach her the Italian and German every Constantinian spoke fluently in so short a time, but he could work a bit on her English. Less rural American and more European, so it would sound better to the average Constantinian ear.

He brought in a former prima ballerina to teach his queen how to walk, how to stand, how to shake hands, and how to curtsy with varying degrees of deference. He made her sit with a selection of his aides and learn the rudiments of the kind of diplomacy she'd be expected to know inside and out at all formal functions. He had yet another aide talk her through the tangled history of Santa Domini and the Constantines, so she would be less likely to trip into any old, festering wounds that still lingered there, as such things tended to do between all ancient European nations. He had her consult with his own public affairs officers, to teach her how to handle cameras and reporters and the unsavory realities of public life in a tabloid world. He even brought in his formidable former nanny, now pushing eighty, to teach Maggy the same excruciatingly correct set of manners she'd taught him back in the day, at the table and everywhere else a royal might venture.

"A banquet is a performance," he heard Madame Rosso pronounce in her usual ringing tones from the formal dining room one afternoon, just as she had when he'd been a boy. "Your appetite has nothing to do with it. Indeed, you must worry about sating yourself on your own time. A banquet is an event at which you are royalty first and a hungry person never. Do you understand?"

"I understand," Maggy said. Sweetly enough that Reza paused outside the room, whatever errand he'd been on forgotten.

She was so understanding when asked anything these days. She always agreed, nodded, curtsied. She modulated her tone and softened her accent. It was as if she'd been possessed by an alien, Reza thought darkly—and the fact he should have been rejoicing over how easily she was taking to what she'd called *Princess School* in a rare flash of her old self one evening made him that much more annoyed with himself.

The truth, and he was all too aware of it, was that he was something far more dangerous than simply *annoyed with himself.*

Reza couldn't quite believe that he found himself missing the sharp-tongued bottle blonde who had looked at him with such blatant disrespect in Vermont. He told himself that of course he didn't. Not really. It was just that Maggy was immersing herself in her studies of all things royal and, in so doing, becoming the princess she'd always been meant to be. The real Maggy would come out the other side, he was sure of it.

Why on earth would you want her to come out

the other side *of decent behavior?* he asked himself then, deeply irritated with his own frailties where this woman was concerned.

But he had no answer for that. The more appropriate she became, the harder he found it to resist her. It was as if the veneer of the princess he'd always wanted stretched over that fearless creature he'd met in Vermont made this woman into his own, personal, walking and talking downfall. No matter how steadfastly he refused to go there.

Meanwhile, he suspected he was a little too insistent about the dinners they shared every night. He told himself that these formal meals were a way to assess her progress. That they were necessary, and perhaps that was true. But he knew full well that wasn't why he found himself anticipating the dinner hour all day.

He was betraying himself and everything he stood for and he couldn't seem to stop.

One night he found her in the grand hall an hour or so before the bell was due to ring to announce dinner. She was counting out loud as she practiced waltzing by herself, her lovely face screwed up into a frown as she stared at her feet and held her arms in a rigid box in the air before her.

It was one thing to want her. That was bad enough. But this...*melting* sensation in the region of his chest was something far worse than simply unacceptable. It was a different sort of danger entirely, he knew it.

And it got worse the more she transformed before him. Tonight it very nearly ached.

Reza ordered himself to move on. To retire to his rooms and dress for dinner the way he knew he should, and maintain the level of formality between them that was the only thing keeping his sanity in check, he sometimes thought.

Instead, he walked into the ballroom.

Maggy was too busy counting to see him approach. "One, two, three, four. One two three four. *Onetwothree—*"

She stopped the moment she saw him. She seemed to freeze into place where she stood, those caramel eyes of hers wide on him, her arms still in the air as if she danced with a ghost.

And he was many things, most of them deeply unsavory at present and entirely too much his father's son, but he was no liar. He knew exactly what that heat was in her gaze. He felt the same thing storm through him, tying him into a thousand intricate knots that felt like fire.

"What are you doing?" she asked. He could tell from that strange tone in her voice that he must look particularly intense.

He should have cared about that. It should have set off every alarm inside of him, that he should betray himself at all, much less so obviously. But if it did, he couldn't bring himself to care.

If this was how his downfall started, he couldn't

seem to mind. Not tonight. Not when she had transformed herself into every last thing he'd always, always wanted.

"Allow me to assist you," he said, his voice dark and low.

Reza didn't wait for her to respond. He had crossed the room by then, so he simply took her in his arms, ignoring the heat that blazed between them.

Well. It was more like he marinated in that heat. Soaked in it. Dared it to try to drown him.

He wrapped his fingers around hers. He liked, too much, her grip on his opposite shoulder. He held her at the correct distance and thought he deserved a medal or ten for refraining from pulling her up hard against his body the way he wanted to do.

And then he started to dance, sweeping her along with him. The fact that there was no music did not signify. There was her breath. There was his heartbeat, hard and deep and needy. Nothing else mattered.

Reza let himself admire her as they moved. His princess. His queen. Tonight her hair was piled on the top of her head, that dark, rich color he preferred, and she was wearing a shift dress that made her look very young and very chic at once. She was still slender, though she'd lost that hungry look over the past weeks. There was nothing at all to distract from her beauty now. Not one single thing.

And he liked having her in his arms almost too much to bear.

"It's hard to reconcile the woman I met in that coffee shop with you now," he said, because he couldn't seem to help himself. He couldn't keep from poking at the very thing he shouldn't touch. "You are so alarmingly agreeable."

"I'm the exact same person," Maggy replied, but he thought her response was too quick. Too pat. And he didn't like that she kept her gaze trained on his chin, as if she was deliberately keeping her eyes from him. Hiding, right there in his arms. "It's just that instead of trying to remember to pay my rent on time, I now have to remember which fork to use."

There was no reason so smooth and rehearsed a response should have bothered him. Reza told himself it didn't. This was what he'd wanted, after all. Indeed, this was what she deserved. She was a royal princess. She *should* appear this way, without any cracks and wholly unobjectionable. His odd nostalgia for the creature she'd become to survive what had happened to her demeaned them both, surely.

He was disgusted with himself. Still, he spun her around the room again and again because he couldn't bring himself to let go. He couldn't make himself do it.

You are a king, said a voice from deep inside of him, sounding very much like his mother's crisp, faintly starchy tones, in those dark days following what they'd all known was his father's suicide to avoid the mess he'd made of his life, his country. *Do you rule or are you ruled?*

He stopped then, abruptly. Maggy's momentum kept her going and she almost fell against him. He almost let her, to serve his own hunger—but at the last moment he righted her.

"I will instruct your dance instructor to pay more attention to your footwork," he heard himself say, his voice like a winter chill. "You cannot trip over foreign dignitaries without causing international incidents."

Her chin rose and she tugged at her hand to get him to release it. He only held it tighter.

"Given that I didn't know how to dance at all until a week or so ago, I think I'm doing fine." Her voice was even, but he was sure he heard a hint of that old fire beneath it.

How sad that he thrilled to it. But he did.

"It is not what you think that matters, Princess." His voice was too low, too telling. But all he could seem to do was stare at the tender place in the hollow of her neck, watching the way her pulse jumped. Reza told himself it could mean anything. That he shouldn't take it as a matching fire, no matter that he could see the echo of it in her gaze. "It is what I think."

He let her go this time when she tugged at her hand again. Maggy stepped back, her chin tilted at that mutinous angle he'd missed far more than he should have, and then, her challenging gaze on his, she executed a crisp and perfect curtsy.

It was perhaps the most eloquent *up yours* gesture he'd ever seen. Certainly directed at him.

"Bravo," he said. He wanted to laugh. But that wasn't the thing that wound tight inside of him, pulling him taut and making him ache. "But I must warn you not to attempt a repeat in front of any other monarch you might encounter. Particularly with all of your attitude on display. You might find yourself beheaded for the insult, and no matter that such things were outlawed centuries ago."

"If that was an insult, I must have learned how to do it wrong," she said, but her caramel eyes gleamed with that same hot challenge when they met his. "My deepest apologies if I offended you, Your Majesty."

And that was the last straw. His title in her mouth, crisp and pointed, as if it was another insult, even as it licked over him like something else entirely.

Reza didn't mean to move. He didn't know he did, but somehow the distance between them was gone, and worse, he had his hands wrapped around the smooth, entrancing place where her upper arms became her shoulders.

He was touching her skin, and not merely her hand. *At last.*

"Reza…" she whispered.

He ignored her. Because he was too close to her, he was *touching* her, and that changed everything.

All these games he'd been playing these last weeks fell away.

There was only this. There was only her.

He thought she said his name again, but it was as if it came from somewhere far away. Lost in the storm that washed through him. His thumbs dragged over her soft skin, back and forth as if he couldn't help himself. He watched, fascinated, as a fresh set of goose bumps rose and then swept across her throat, giving her away. Telling him everything he needed to know.

"You cannot taunt me with your brand-new manners and then take it back with my name, Princess," he told her, bending his head toward hers. "You cannot imagine that will work."

Her hands were flat against his chest, but she didn't push against him. Her fingers seemed to curl in, as if she was trying to find purchase against his jacket. As if she wanted to hold on to him.

And her full, lush mouth was *right there* within reach.

Reza stopped pretending he had any control left. He stopped pretending he could resist her when that resistance had grown more and more scant with every passing day.

He stopped pretending, full stop.

He damned himself fully, and then he took her mouth with his.

CHAPTER SEVEN

HIS MOUTH WAS as hard as it looked. Uncompromising and stern as it moved on hers, taking her and tasting her, encouraging her to do the same.

And when she did, when she met him, his taste filled her. Hot and ruthless and entirely Reza.

It was glorious. It was better than glorious.

This is no dream, something inside her whispered. *This is the fairy-tale kiss to end all fairy-tale kisses, and it's real.*

But for once, Maggy didn't care either way. She just wanted more.

She gave herself over to his demanding mouth. His kiss was heat and light, pouring into her and through her, kicking up fires wherever it touched. Her heart cartwheeled in her chest. Her head spun around and around. Her breasts seemed to swell with all the hunger that stormed through her, her nipples pulled to tight points, and between her legs she was nothing but a soft, molten ache.

His hands gripped her upper arms, firm and sure, and lifted her closer to him. And there wasn't a single thought in Maggy's entire being except *yes. More.* More of Reza. More of that stern, hard mouth. More of this wild, stirring electric hunger that tore through her, making her greedy and half-mad. Making her entirely his, as if this right here was where she truly belonged.

She wanted more.

Maggy surged up on her toes and she dug her fingers into the stone wall of his chest, and that was when he angled his mouth for a deeper, better fit.

And the world exploded.

All the heat and fire of these past weeks, all the sensation and need and longing, burst through her. He claimed her mouth, again and again, merciless and almost too hot to bear, and she couldn't seem to get close enough.

Maggy wanted more. She wanted everything.

He made a low noise she didn't recognize, but still it rolled through her and made her even warmer, as if there was some deep, feminine part of her that understood him in ways the rest of her couldn't.

She had always kept a part of her separate, no matter what, but here, now, in his arms, she melted. He kissed her again and again, and she met him with everything she was and everything inside of her and all the wildfire and yearning she'd been pretending wasn't there and Maggy knew, somehow, that there was no going back from this.

A princess was one thing. She could play that part, apparently. She even liked it.

But he kissed her as if she was the woman she'd always wanted to become.

As if she was truly his.

Very much as if he heard that dangerous thought inside her head—as if she'd shouted it out into the empty ballroom—Reza wrenched his mouth from hers. So fast and so unexpected that for a head-spinning moment, Maggy thought maybe she really had said it out loud.

Which would have been a disaster. She knew that. Having feelings for Reza could only complicate everything. Even this. Maybe especially this.

Would any of this have happened if you didn't *have feelings for him already?* an arch voice inside her asked. She ignored it.

His breath sawed out between them as if he'd been running, or maybe that was hers—she couldn't tell. But he didn't let go. His hands were strong and elegant at once, and he kept them wrapped tight around her upper arms.

Maggy knew she should have felt trapped. But she didn't. She felt safer than she could remember ever feeling before, and it didn't matter that the look on his face was anything but sweet.

"This cannot happen," he gritted out.

He was still holding her to him. His face, so harsh and fierce and stern and beautiful, was close to hers. And Maggy was plastered up against him, her breasts pressed to his chest, so hard she could feel her own nipples like twin points of fire where they brushed against him.

She should have been upset, surely. She should certainly have disliked his tone. She should have been…something. But instead she couldn't think of a single place she'd rather be than right here in his arms, no matter how or why or what intense reaction he was having to it.

"I thought you intended to marry me," she whispered, from that same, strange place she hadn't known was there, feminine and wise. She'd never flirted in her life. Why put something out there if she didn't care enough to mean it? But here, now, she tilted her head back and arched into him, smiling when his breath caught. "How will you manage that if we don't do this?"

He set her back from him then, and that felt like a much greater loss than it should have, surely. It felt as if he'd kicked her. For a moment she swayed as if she might topple over, so badly did every part of her want to be close to him again. Closer. The distance between them felt like a slap.

But yeah, that voice inside her poked at her. *Good thing you don't have any* feelings *for him.*

His gray gaze was so dark it looked nearly black.

"Our marriage will be based on civility and respect," he grated at her, and he didn't sound like the Reza she knew at all. There was no distance there. No regal *certainty.* Something inside her prickled to awareness. "Not this…relentless hunger."

Maggy tilted her head to one side, then folded her arms over her chest, and who cared if her deportment instructor had forbidden her to do that. Repeatedly.

"I hate to break this to you, Reza," she said quietly. She realized as she spoke that she had no idea where her sense of calm came from. As if her body knew, way down deep inside, that she was safer here than she'd ever been anywhere else. Here, with him. No matter what was making him look at her that way. "But heirs are not made out of civility and respect. That sounds more like a handshake, which, unless it's different for kings, won't quite get the job done."

"This is who I am." His voice was even more ragged, his gray eyes were more storm than rain, and Maggy stared. That was temper on his face, she was sure of it. Dark and furious. And with something else beneath that she understood instinctively, though she couldn't name it. She felt it inside her, like a new heat. "There is absolutely no place in my life for this kind of distraction."

"By *this kind of distraction*, do you mean a wife? Or a queen?" She studied him. "Or are you talking about a kiss?"

And then she watched him change, right there

before her. She watched him beat back the storm and close himself off, one breath to the next. It was as if he rolled himself up tight into an armored ball. She watched his expression clear, then go cold. His gaze lightened, his mouth firmed. He stood straighter, somehow, and that intense, ruthless power that seemed to blaze straight out from inside him filled the whole of the ballroom.

This was the king of the Constantines in all his glory. But Maggy had kissed the man. She wanted him back. She wanted the storm.

She wanted to dance in it.

"You have taken to your role admirably," he told her, back to that stern, stuffy tone that she knew she should hate. She knew it. But instead it pulled taut inside of her, fire and need. "I anticipate we will be ready to introduce you to the world sooner rather than later."

"Do kings not kiss?" she asked mildly, in a provoking sort of tone her former employers and battalions of counselors would have used to prove her attitude was eternally bad. "I didn't realize that was a breach of royal protocol."

He looked at her with that arrogant astonishment she remembered from the coffee shop. But something had changed—inside her. She could see that same expression. She remembered how she'd felt about it the first time—or how she'd told herself she felt. But now it was like a lit flame, burning her from the inside out.

"I beg your pardon?"

It might have been phrased as a question, even if he used that scaldingly remote and royally outraged tone. It wasn't one.

Maggy shrugged. Deliberately. "You seem so..." She waved a hand at him, not quite as dismissive as his, but certainly a contender. "Upset. I thought maybe there was some royal proclamation forbidding the kingly lips from touching another's."

That muscle in his jaw clenched tight. "There is not."

"Then it's me that's the issue." She eyed him. "Is that what you're trying to tell me? That you have a problem with trailer trash after all? Even after all these weeks of playing Henry Higgins, just for me?"

Reza seemed to expand, hard and harsh, to fill the room, though he didn't move. Maggy could *feel* him everywhere. Pressing against her. Temper and divine right like a fog that stole inside and clogged the whole of the chamber.

"I will see you at dinner at the appointed time," he told her, his voice so cold she was surprised icicles didn't form. "We will discuss the history of the Constantines and the Santa Dominian line of succession."

She managed, somehow, to keep her expression blank. "That sounds thrilling."

His jaw looked tight enough to shatter. "We will

never mention this unfortunate episode again, so allow me to make this clear now. You are not *trailer trash*. You are the daughter of a revered and ancient bloodline. And for the record, I do not have problems with anyone or anything. I solve problems or am otherwise above the fray, as is appropriate for a man in my position."

"Is that why you're so grumpy after a little kiss?" Maggy smiled at him when he glared at her, and she'd gotten a whole lot better at smiling since she'd come here. She was almost good at it now. "Because you're so above it?"

She thought he meant to say something. That perfect mouth of his moved and his dark gray eyes flashed, but he didn't speak. He merely inclined his head in that coolly dismissive way of his. Then he turned on his heel with military precision and marched from the room.

Maggy stood where he left her. She made herself breathe, deep and long, to get the shakiness out. Her mouth felt slightly swollen, sweetly battered from his, and she indulged herself, there in the middle of a fairy-tale ballroom on a faraway island, by pressing her fingers against her own lips. As if she could conjure up his kiss again that easily.

The truth was, everything had changed tonight. She thought he knew it, too, or why else would he have reacted that way? All this time, she'd told herself that she was happy to go along with this because it got her out of her hard, cold, empty grind and allowed her to live the sort of storybook life she'd tried so hard to stop letting herself dream because it was too painful every time she woke up. Because doing this meant she belonged somewhere, and she could never be rejected from a place she claimed with her blood. She'd told herself that was all that mattered.

But she'd been lying to herself. It had been as much about Reza as it had been about her remarkably stubborn princess dreams and the reality of that blood test. Maybe more.

She'd agreed to marry *him*, not a fairy tale. She'd left everything she knew because he'd come and found her. *Him*. Not some random person. Not one of the tabloid reporters who dogged the steps of every royal in Europe. Not the brother she was still coming to terms with having in the first place.

And she'd thrown herself headfirst into this crash course in becoming something other than trailer trash, which Maggy knew she'd been all her life no matter what he said to the contrary. No one in the foster care system had cared too much about her *ancient bloodline*. She hadn't done all this because she was particularly fired up about being a queen. Or even because the clothes were exquisite and she'd discovered things about herself she'd never have known before and would never have found out—like the fact emeralds didn't suit her, she preferred Louboutins to Jimmy Choos, and had an abiding appreciation for a very particular bath salt her attendants told her was handmade in one specific boutique in Bali. That was all its own delight, to be sure.

But deep down, if she was brutally honest with herself, she'd been trying her hardest to make herself into the kind of woman Reza wanted.

Maybe it wasn't even that deep down.

Every night she sat at the table in the formal dining room and turned herself inside out trying to make that ruthless mouth of his soften, just a little bit. Every night she trotted out pertinent facts and used the right utensils to show she was learning her numerous lessons. She sat with elegant posture and made the sort of easy and yet sophisticated conversation she'd been told—repeatedly—set a woman who would be queen apart from the masses. Educated and yet wry, compelling and yet not overly opinionated.

"The formal dinner table is no place for strong opinions," Madame Rosso told her again and again.

"Because heaven forbid it put a man off his food," Maggy had muttered once, glaring mulishly at the empty plate before her, several hours into a crash course on formal manners.

The king's former nanny had fixed her with a frank stare, all the way down the impressive length of her nose, the force of it making the white hair piled on top of her head seem to wobble.

"This is about diplomacy," she'd said in her crisp, clear-eyed way. "You are a royal princess. You will not be dining with people rounded up off the streets who might be in any doubt about the issues of the day. It is likely, in fact, that you will be seated with those who decide those issues. And when policy is served in the middle of a meal, it can only cause indigestion. A meal is the time one behaves as if the world is already perfect, war and strife do not exist, and everyone near you is a close, personal friend."

"Because no one needs to hear the opinion of a princess." Maggy had wrinkled up her nose. "I get it."

"Because the point of a princess is that you are a symbol," Madame Rosso had returned, her tone faintly chiding. "You are an amiable and benevolent reminder of what is for many a bygone time. It is called being gracious, Your Highness. In public, it is your greatest weapon. In private, of course, one expects you will have no trouble whatsoever making your opinions known however you choose and to whomever you wish."

And Maggy discovered that, in fact, she *wanted* to be gracious. She wanted to be a symbol of something positive as opposed to the poster child for neglect. She wanted to make this new role of hers her own in every possible way.

But most of all, she wanted to be Reza's.

Maggy could finally admit it, with her mouth still tingling from his mercilessly beautiful kiss. She wanted to be *his*.

She'd assumed that inhabiting the role of perfect princess was the way to do it, because that was what he'd said he needed from her, or wanted for her. The perfect princess, then the perfect queen. And all that entailed—heirs and grace and whatever else. But that was before he'd kissed her. That was before she'd seen that storm in him and wanted nothing more than to bathe in it.

That was before he'd claimed her mouth with his and brought her alive. Wickedly, deliciously, beautifully *alive*. More alive than she'd ever been before in all her life.

Which meant, she realized as she stood there in that ballroom filled with need and longing and *Reza* long after he'd left it, she needed to come up with a different plan.

Two nights later, after a series of such excruciatingly stiff meals she was surprised she hadn't turned to stone in the middle of them, Maggy decided it was time she tested the waters. He'd called what happened between them *a relentless hunger*. She wanted to see just how hungry he really was.

Because it turned out she was ravenous.

After another long, stiff dinner packed with a barrage of dry facts and the king's dark glower from across the exquisitely set table, they moved into one of the many salons that littered the villa. Reza chose a different one every night, but what happened in each was always the same. They would sit and talk about things even more innocuous than what had passed for dinner table conversation.

"This is ridiculous," she'd said on one of the first nights they'd done this, scowling at him. "I'm not going to tell you what I did in the summers while I was growing up. Why would you want to know?"

"This is called a conversation," he'd replied, his expression like granite, though she'd been sure she'd seen a hint of that silvery gleam in his gaze. Or maybe she'd just wanted it there, more than was probably healthy. "It is much like dancing. It is all about the appearance of being light and airy, the better to put the person you are speaking with at his ease."

"If the person I'm speaking with isn't at his ease after nine hundred courses and too much dessert, I don't think me sitting here making up pleasant lies about my summertime activities is going to help."

"You are not required to lie."

"Oh, okay." She'd glared at him, but she'd remembered to fold her hands in her lap so at least she looked like a lady while she did it. "I'd be happy to tell you about the summer I worked in the convenience store because I wanted to save up enough money to buy myself new shoes for school in the fall. My foster mother stole it from under my bed and spent it all on booze. Or wait, maybe the time the only job I could get was as a waitress in a sleazy motel restaurant, but the manager fired me because I wouldn't have sex with him. Or I know, the summer I got a great job in a cute boutique on Main Street, but they let me go because I didn't have a car and it took me so long to walk there every morning that I was always a sweaty mess when I arrived. That just wasn't the trendy boutique look they were going for, you see."

"You've made your point." His voice had been silken reproval, all the way through. She'd ignored it.

"What did you do in your summers?" she'd asked him. "Polish the crown jewels? Behead a few peasants for a little giggle? Use your scepter as a machete as the mood took you?"

"My summers were devoted to charity work," he'd said, surprising her more than she wanted to admit. "A different charity every summer from the time I was ten. Usually in a different country and for a different cause, and all of them quite hands-on. Many sick children, I'm afraid, though I also spent some time digging ditches. I was not raised to be the vicious and selfish monarch you seem to imagine." His brows rose. "Beheadings and machetes and the crown jewels do not figure strongly under my rule, you might be surprised to learn."

"I thought that was the point of being king," she'd said, but the edge had gone from the conversation. She'd seen that silver gleam in his gaze, the one that made her feel warm all over.

"The point of the kind of light, easy conversation

we have after dinner is twofold," he'd told her after a moment. She'd become fixated on his hands then. The way he held one of them in the air as he lounged in his chair, looking as if he sat on a high throne instead of in an armchair. "First, it is happy. Sparkling. It allows you to guide the room in whichever direction you choose. And second, it is more intimate. Guests will have eaten, perhaps have had too much to drink. It is highly likely this is where deeper topics will be discussed—but that won't happen if we all sit about in silence."

She'd looked at him. "I'm a diversion, then?"

He hadn't quite smiled. "My mother once held a room filled with men on the brink of war spellbound as she waxed rhapsodic about the balls she'd attended as a young woman. It was silly talk, but she made them laugh. It allowed my father to have a much needed casual aside with a man known at that time as the Butcher of the Balkans, and after that, the drums of war beat a little more quietly." He'd swirled something amber in his glass for a moment before fixing her with that fathomless gray stare. "Never underestimate the importance of that diversion, Princess."

Tonight, they settled into Maggy's favorite salon after their meal, which she decided was a good omen. It was an old study that felt more like a cozy library than a chilly sitting room. There was an ancient globe on a stand that had all the wrong names on countries with borders that had shifted a long time since. Hardbound books with gold-edged pages lined the walls. The fire was bright and warm tonight, holding the stormy winter weather outside at bay.

Maggy liked the rain against all the windows. It made her think of that hunger Reza had talked about. It made her feel it everywhere, roaring inside of her. Making her feel far braver than perhaps she should.

Reza was talking about something so light and so far removed from what she was thinking that she didn't pretend to follow it. He'd given her a glass of something as sweet as it was alcoholic, but she'd only tasted it once before putting it aside. She was after something else entirely tonight.

It took her a long moment to realize that Reza had stopped speaking. That the room had gone silent. That there was no sound at all save the fire crackling and spitting against the grate, and outside, the winter storm rattling the windows. That Reza's gaze was on hers, all that dark gray unreadable. If not outright forbidding.

Trouble was, it didn't intimidate her. She liked him granite and imposing. She thought the truth was, she liked *him*. Full stop.

"I apologize." He was quite obviously not sorry. That was clear from his tone, not to mention that frigid, regal expression on his face. "Am I boring you?"

Maggy stood then, trying to remember how to

be graceful the way she'd been taught. She ran her hands down the front of her gown, a sweet fall of dark blue silk that brushed the floor despite the high shoes she wore. And any nerves she might have had now that she was really doing this—and she was really, truly doing this, no matter what—were swept away by the way Reza tracked the movement. As if he couldn't quite help himself. As if he wanted it to be *his* hands on her like that.

That was what she wanted to find out. If he did. If he wanted her as much as she wanted him.

If that kiss had been a mistake—or if it was the new beginning between them that it had felt like to her.

"I want to thank you," she told him.

He was lounging in yet another armchair, the way he always did. How he managed to give the impression of slumping without actually doing so was a marvel, she thought. A bit of royal magic. He'd opened the jacket of yet another perfect suit— and Maggy knew enough now to understand that the word for the kind of hand-tooled clothing he preferred was *bespoke*. That he had many such suits, all made to his precise specifications and all, like this one, a love song to his hard, solid, sculpted body.

She wanted to know the words to that song. Then she wanted to sing it.

Reza said nothing, and that was almost more alarming than all the cutting things he could have said. He only watched her as she moved toward him, though she could feel the weight of it, as if his gray gaze really was the hard, pounding rain that washed over the windows behind him. He remained silent when she came to stand before him, just inside the V of his outthrust legs.

"You've given me everything," she told him.

And even though she'd planned this to be light and airy, the way everyone kept teaching her these royal games of intrigue over waltzes and dinners and after dinner drinks were meant to be, it didn't sound that way when she said it. It occurred to her, once the words were out, that it was no less than the raw and simple truth.

Oh, well, she thought. *No use pretending now.*

She made herself continue. "I want to give you something in return."

"You will give me your hand in marriage soon enough." His voice was too low and a bit too rough, but he was watching her with a certain alertness that made her blood seem to quicken inside her veins. It encouraged her even as it moved in her like a deep, sweet caress. And most importantly, he didn't order her to step away from him. Or to take her seat again. "That is more than sufficient."

"I can't possibly give you any kind of gift you don't already have," she told him. Her heart was pounding inside her chest. Her eyes felt glassy. "So

I thought instead I would give you something I've never given anyone else. Ever."

Something in his gray gaze changed then, like a new storm washing out the old. That hard mouth of his moved. "Princess. That isn't necessary."

But she had no intention of heeding that warning she heard in his voice. She wanted this too much. She wanted *him* too much. And she'd spent a lifetime refusing to allow herself to want things she couldn't have.

She didn't want to do it any longer. It felt like defeat, and that was a part of her old life. This was her new start. *He* was her new life.

Maggy wanted to taste every bit of it, starting with him.

She gathered up all her courage and every last bit of that greedy, ravenous hunger that stormed through her now and, if she was being as honest with herself as possible, had since he'd walked through the coffee shop door and she'd thought he was *extraordinary*. She still did. That made it easy to sink down on her knees before him, until she was kneeling up between his legs.

"Maggy."

She liked her name on his lips, and no matter the tone he used—just this side of a command. She liked the arrested, *aware* look on his harsh face and, even more, the way it shivered all through her, as if that silver gleam was inside her, too.

She shifted forward so she could put her hands on his thighs, then run them up toward his lap, her goal obvious.

Maggy thought of the coffee shop again, and how she'd thought he'd seemed like a man who was used to having people on their knees before him. Had she wanted to do this even then? Her mouth watered at the thought.

Reza didn't move. If anything, he got *more* still, as if he really did turn to stone beneath her hands. But it was a hot, masculine sort of stone. It made her belly seem to twist into a complicated knot, then sink down between her legs. Maggy tipped her head back so she could keep her eyes on his. Too much gray and too much silver besides, and when that muscle clenched in his jaw, she felt it in her core, molten and greedy.

She slid her hands up farther, reveling in the feel of his strong, corded thighs beneath her palms. All his power. All that heat. She sensed more than saw the way his hands gripped the arms of his chair.

"Maggy."

The way he said her name was supposed to stop her. She understood that. But he didn't actually order her to stop.

So she didn't.

She paused for the faintest moment at the top of his thighs, where she could see his hard length against his fly—growing larger and more fascinating the longer she sat there and looked at it. She slid her hands up farther still, only grazing the front of his fly in passing as she reached for his belt.

He jolted as if he would reach to stop her—but he didn't.

The sound of his buckle seemed louder than it should. Ruder and more delicious with only the snap of the fire behind it. Maggy felt herself flush, but she couldn't stop now. She was too close. Her breath kept tangling in her throat and between her legs, she felt a matching rush of sensation.

Molten heat, soft and wild, and all for him.

She pulled his trousers open, her heart punching at her hard. So hard it made her stomach flip over and over. Her hands trembled slightly. She didn't know which was worse, the longing that made her knees feel soft and weak beneath her or the panic that he might stop her at any moment when she was this close. When she was finally so close.

She reached into the opening she'd made and pulled out the hardest part of him, wrapping her fingers around the thick, hard length. She swallowed, hard, and looked up at him as she indulged herself, moving her hand all the way down to his root, his silken smoothness against her palm making her whole body shake with need.

His face was set, that muscle in his jaw something like ferocious. He was so fierce, so harsh, he should have scared her—but he didn't. He never had. She understood that glitter in his gaze now, the way she had the other night when he'd kissed her. She felt it racing through her, making her feel clumsy and needy and maddened with this same hunger.

And she knew that whatever else happened, however stony he became, he wanted her exactly as much as she wanted him.

The knowledge felt like safety. Like freedom. Like both at once, wrapped up together and indistinguishable from one another.

Maggy wrapped her free hand around him, too. Then she tipped herself forward, kept her gaze on his as she opened her mouth, and sucked him in deep.

CHAPTER EIGHT

REZA DIDN'T KNOW how he didn't embarrass himself on the spot.

Maggy's hot, clever mouth closed over him, the world exploded into bright red need and a mad rush of pure lust, and he was nearly lost.

Nearly.

She took him deeper. She wrapped her fingers around the base of him and she tested his length against her tongue. She pulled back and lavished attention on the broad head before sucking him back in again.

She'd said she'd never done this before, and he was amazed at how...primitive that made him. How possessive.

He thought her inexpert attempt to please him with her sheer enthusiasm and that hot, wet mouth of hers might actually kill him.

But if this was how he was going to die, Reza thought it might be worth it. He kept his hands fisted hard on the arms of his chair. He let her play with him, her dark hair swirling around her bare shoulders and moving over his thighs like heat. He watched in dark fascination and that same red-hot greed as she took him deeper. Then deeper still.

He felt her everywhere.

And he had never wanted anyone or anything more.

He knew that should have alarmed him, that razor's edge of desire that was a bit too close to desperation. He knew what indulging in this, in her, made him. He knew he should push her off, reclaim his control, insist on all the cold, clear boundaries that had to stand between them or everything else would shatter—

But he couldn't do it.

He didn't *want* to do it.

Reza wanted her. *Her*. He wanted his princess, his queen, the woman who had been promised to him at her birth. The girl he'd lost before she'd had a chance to grow up into his woman. The future that had been wrenched away from him when he'd only just become a man. He wanted the queen he'd mourned throughout his twenties.

He wanted the real, live, insanely beautiful woman who knelt before him and *thanked him* with every blazingly slick slide of her smart, hot mouth along the hardest, neediest part of him. Again and again and again.

And he had already damned himself when he'd

kissed her in that ballroom. Why not enjoy the flames?

All the lies Reza had told himself since he'd seen that photograph with his own lost princess bride in the background, all the walls he'd built since then and tried to keep solid, all the thousands of ways he'd pretended he could maintain his boundaries against this woman who had been born to be his, the power she wielded over him because she was his lost Magdalena and because she was his Maggy besides—it all simply crumbled around him.

And Reza found he didn't much care, because in the wreckage there was still her, his princess, knelt there between his legs with her mouth against him, driving him straight toward that cliff.

"No," he bit out, aware of the harshness of his voice only once he heard himself, the echo of his furious, ungovernable hunger rough in the quiet of the room.

Maggy froze, pulling her mouth free of him while her hands were still wrapped tight around him. But even that was too much. Reza muttered out something in Italian, a curse or a prayer and he didn't know which, reaching down to pull her off of him before he lost his last little shred of control. He eased her up from between his legs even as he moved out of the chair, sliding down to the floor to kneel there with her.

Then he took her face—her exquisite, impossible face, intelligent and lovely and *his*—between his hands.

"Reza," she whispered, her hands moving to curl around his wrists. "I want—"

"*I* want," he corrected her gruffly. "And believe me, Princess, I intend to have what I want. Everything I want."

And then he took her mouth with his, and let that bright red desire for her wash over him. He couldn't taste her deeply enough. He couldn't hold her close enough. He angled his jaw, tangling his tongue with hers. He indulged that sharp greed inside of him, letting one hand move to fist in her thick hair while the other learned that delicious arch of her back, then settled on the sweet curve of her bottom.

It wasn't enough. Reza feasted on her mouth the way he'd wanted to forever, and even more since that kiss in the ballroom. She shivered as she kissed him back, rubbing her breasts against his chest as if she was as desperate as he was. As needy. As impatient.

And everything had changed tonight.

The brakes were off. The walls were down.

There were so many reasons he shouldn't do this—but chief among them was the fact that with Maggy in his arms, her mouth beneath his again, and her lush, lean body pressed against him, he couldn't think of a single one of them.

To hell with the king of the Constantines. Tonight he was nobody but Reza.

With Maggy that felt like a revelation instead of a disaster.

He lost himself in her taste. The scent of her skin, vanilla and coconut, as if she was a touch of the tropics in the middle of the winter storm outside. The sheer, dizzying perfection of her mouth against his and the way her taste inflamed him and wrecked him, over and over again.

Reza lost himself in sensation. In her. In the perfection that was his lost princess, finally found. Finally exactly where she'd been meant to be all along.

He let his hands move over her again, restlessly testing her curves and making her moan into his mouth. He trailed a line of fire and need down the length of her elegant neck, learning every inch of her and where a lick or a graze of his teeth made her shudder. He bent to taste the plump, smooth thrust of her breasts above the bodice of her dress and in the mad fire of that he took her down with him to the soft, thick rug.

And then she was beneath him, her caramel eyes shining and her mouth faintly damp from his. *Finally.* Reza remembered her down on her knees in that coffee shop, staring at him as if he was an unwelcome intrusion. He remembered her soft and asleep on his shoulder in the back of the SUV, so vulnerable and so trusting at once. He could still feel her mouth all over the length of him, while the taste of her rocketed through him and made him something like thirsty.

She was his. Here, now she was entirely his. *At last.*

Her gaze was wide. Dark with the same need that moved in him. Her hair was a dark cloud around her, gleaming in the firelight, and it took everything he had to hold himself there for a moment, up on his elbows above her. As if he needed to etch this moment into his memory forever. Maggy reached up and pushed his jacket off his shoulders and he let her do it, tossing it aside as soon as possible. And then he hissed out a breath when she went further, reaching up beneath the tail of his shirt to get her hands on his skin.

It was like fire. It was better than fire. Her hands were a torment and a blessing as one traced its way up his spine and the other moved lower to test his backside against her palm.

He needed to be closer to her. He needed…everything.

"I need to be inside you," he gritted out, and he was too far gone to care that he sounded wrecked. Like a stranger to himself. Like a man with no brakes, no control, nothing.

Like a man, not a king.

It should have stopped him dead. But Maggy was clinging to him, her mouth to his.

"I need that, too," she whispered. "I need you, Reza."

And everything shifted then. It got hotter. Wilder. Deeper red and far more intense.

Reza reached between them and pulled her filmy, silken dress up and out of his way with rather more intent than finesse. He didn't care that he'd lost all his ease and grace and caution, not when her smooth, sculpted legs were bared to his gaze. He ran his hand up, growling his appreciation of her taut thigh and continuing until he reached the tiny little scrap of silk and lace between her legs.

He held himself above her, his gaze hard and greedy on hers, as he stroked his way beneath that little scrap and found her scalding heat at last.

She shivered beneath him as he tested her with one finger. Two. So hot and soft. He thought she might kill him and he couldn't think, just then, of a better way to go than wrapped up tight in all her molten heat.

"Maggy—" he began, but he didn't know what he meant to say. Maybe he'd simply needed her name on his lips.

"Please." Her voice was stark. Greedy. Her gaze was dark and glassy at once, and she was writhing beneath him, every part of her a sweet, scalding invitation. "Please, Reza."

"Use your hands," he ordered her, low and sure. "Guide me in, Princess. Take me deep."

He felt the way she jolted against him at his words.

He saw the fire dance over her face, making her gaze a gleaming thing, over-bright and needy.

Then her hands were on him again, a torment and a glory. She wrapped her fingers around his aching length, raising her hips to him as she did as he'd commanded and guided him toward her entrance, using one hand to rake her panties to one side. Reza bent to take her mouth as she lifted herself up, impaling herself on him. He slid one hand around to hold her bottom where he wanted her, and then he thrust into her. Deeper and then deeper still, too hungry, too greedy, to wait the extra seconds it would take to undress either one of them any further.

And when he was buried to the hilt, they both froze, their eyes locked to each other. His whole length snug inside of her, deep and hard.

The whole world narrowed down to this. Here. The two of them.

His princess. His queen. At last.

"Please…" she whispered. Again. And he thought he'd never heard a prettier sound than his tough little princess begging him.

Reza began to move.

It was throwing himself into an inferno, again and again and again. It was a wild taking. A deep, greedy possession.

It was perfect. *She* was perfect.

She wrapped herself around him and Reza couldn't get close enough. Deep enough. He couldn't taste her enough. Her wicked mouth. Her sweetly elegant neck. Her gorgeous, ripe little breasts.

He wondered if anything would ever be enough when it came to this woman. Even this.

Right here, right now, he didn't care.

And then suddenly, it was too much. He felt his control go liquid, and it took everything he had to haul himself back from that edge even as he maintained his hard, deep pace.

He reached between them and found the very center of her need. He rubbed her there, keeping his strokes deep and hard.

"Come for me," he growled against her neck.

And she obeyed him. She clenched against him and she shuddered all around him, then cried out his name as she fell.

And Reza followed her straight over the side of the world.

Outside the villa, the winter storm raged on through the night.

But Maggy was far more interested in the one she was caught up in with Reza, inside, where it was dry but not quite safe. Not when there were so many things to discover about him. And so many things he could do to her.

She wanted to do every single one of them.

When she came back into herself, there on the floor of the study, she felt wrecked—but in a beautiful, glorious way. As if her skin could hardly hold all the things she felt inside.

Reza lifted himself above her, his face dark. Unreadable.

And for a moment it was hard to tell where the rain outside ended and he began.

Then he lifted his hand and brought it to her face, stroking down her jaw. As if she was precious to him. As if he cared—

Maggy knew that was foolish. That she was only going to hurt herself, thinking such things about a man like him, so ruthless and mighty above all else.

She thought he would say something then. She thought he would go out of his way to remind her that he was a king and she was beneath him the way everyone else he encountered was beneath him. That he held all the power here, one way or another.

But he didn't say a word.

After a long moment lost in his endless gray gaze, Reza pulled out of her and rolled away. She hardly had time to process the loss of his silken and steel length within her, his hard body against her, his heat all around her, because he was standing then. He rose from the floor to his feet in an unconscious show of all that forbidding grace that made him who he was. He hauled up his trousers and fastened them, then looked down at her where she still lay there, spread out on the thick rug on the floor of the salon.

Boneless.

Something moved over his face, too quick for her to read, and then he held out his hand.

It reminded her of the coffee shop, and Maggy didn't know how she felt about that. Only that it seemed to trigger something raw and unwieldy inside of her, swamping her where she lay. She sat up, trying to fight it off, tugging her dress back down to cover her legs.

And Reza merely waited there, his hand extended, as if he could do so all night.

The only reason you're hesitating to take his hand is that you're too eager and you don't want him to know it, she told herself caustically.

She decided that was stupid. She'd already proved her eagerness with her mouth. What was the point of pretending otherwise now? She'd already given herself away entirely. There was no going back.

Maggy held out her hand and let him lift her to her feet. Then he hauled her against him. He kept tugging until she was off balance, and then he simply bent at the knees and swept her up into his arms.

"Reza," she began, high against his chest with that unsmiling mouth of his *right there* and his harshly compelling face *so close*—

He didn't so much as glance at her as he started to move.

"Hush," he murmured as he shouldered his way out of the study and started down the long hall toward their rooms. "Not tonight."

Maggy took that as gospel.

He carried her through the dimly lit villa, and Maggy did nothing but wrap one arm around his neck and let him take her where he liked. She had only passing impressions of rooms with lights on and flickering candles in the sconces along the ancient walls. She saw the door to her own room as they passed it, and let a breath out then, resting her head against his strong shoulder.

Inside his suite, Reza moved quickly through the private salon where he'd stood with her before that tilted mirror. He carried her down another hall that was more like a paneled foyer, past what looked like an office and another, even more private study. She lifted her head from his shoulder when he entered yet another room, then kicked the door closed behind him.

There was a vast stone fireplace on one wall, taking over the whole of that side of the room with a fire dancing cheerfully in its grate. It was the only light in the bedchamber. She saw a few chairs and a sofa arranged before it, but then he was lifting her up and placing her on a vast, supremely kingly bed. Four stout, carved columns rose in each corner, but there was no canopy here to relieve the male stamp of it. Only acres of mattress and soft linens in dark, brooding colors.

And Maggy didn't care about any of that. She cared about the man who stood at the side of the wide, high bed, his glittering gaze fixed on her while the firelight played all over him and made him look more like a myth than a man.

He didn't speak.

And that look on his face was so intent, so fierce, that Maggy followed suit.

Reza undressed her carefully. His hard hands smoothed over her ankles and unbuckled the delicate straps of her shoes, then tugged them off. He found the fastening to her gown at its side and pulled the zipper down, then lifted her to sweep the dress away. His gaze glittered hot when he looked at her then, in nothing but the tiny panties she'd held to one side before, but he didn't haul her to him. He only hooked his fingers in the lacy sides of the panties and slid them down, then off.

When she was naked, he looked at her for a long, long while. He raked his fingers through her hair, almost as if he was arranging it to suit himself. Then he let his hands wander, testing her collarbone with one finger. Then finding her nipples with his thumbs while he lifted her breasts into his hard palms.

He leaned in then, putting his lips over one nipple and sucking until it hardened against his tongue. By the time he made his lazy way to her other nipple, she was shivering again, that same fire lit again inside of her and burning bright.

Reza stepped back then, and Maggy pushed herself up to her knees so she could watch him as he rid himself of his clothes with a certain ferocity that made that knot low in her belly pulse. Then glow.

When he was naked, Maggy heard herself let out a reverent sort of sigh that she could no more keep inside than she could have stopped herself from getting on her knees earlier.

He was beautiful. He was made of hard planes and delectable ridges, all lean muscle and corded, male power.

Reza crawled onto the bed with her, one arm around her middle to shift her into the center of the mattress.

"Reza…" she tried again, because the wild, raw hollow inside of her was growing, pushing everything else aside, caught in the storm of sensation. His thighs were a rough delight against hers. She could feel him again, hard and insistent, against the soft skin of her belly. And he was settled on his elbows above her, his fingers deep in her hair.

"Quiet, Princess," he murmured. "This is a time for action, not words."

And then he took her mouth with his, showing her exactly what he meant.

He tasted her everywhere. He spread fire and need everywhere he went. He explored her body, inch by inch, tasting her and touching her, then flipping her over so he could do the same to her other side. His mouth moved down the length of her spine, torturously slow, and she felt his hard mouth curve against her skin when he made her shudder.

By the time he turned her over again she was making no attempt to hide her moans, her pleading. His face was dark as he came over her, his eyes nearly black with passion.

And when he slid into her, she burst apart, sensation shattering her into a thousand pieces.

"Beautiful," he murmured as she shook and shook, her fingers pressed deep into his back. "You are so beautiful, my Magdalena."

Then he began to move.

Slow. Lazy.

Unbearably hot.

He rode her, sweet and easy, through her shattering, then kept on going, tossing her from one peak straight into a brand-new fire.

He played with her mouth, her breasts. He acted as if he had all the time in the world. And when she started to lift her hips to meet him again, when that tension wound around and around inside of her and made her cling to him and arch into his thrusts, he let himself go.

Reza gathered her close and pounded into her, every drag of his hips throwing her closer and closer and closer still, until she broke again, flying apart into scraps of fire and need and something far greater than either.

And she held him tight as he followed her, shouting out her name.

It took a long, long time for him to stir, and when he did, his gaze came to hers in the flickering light. Maggy had to bite her lip to keep back the things that threatened to spill over then. The truths she hadn't wanted to face but could hardly avoid now, naked with him like this.

She didn't know what he saw on her face. But he still didn't speak. He rolled them over again, and this time, he carried her to his bathroom. He set her down in a huge, glassed-in enclosure, and then he washed her, his expression serious.

When they were both squeaky clean, he took her back to that great big bed and climbed into it with her, arranging her so she was draped over his body, and Maggy thought it was the perfect time to say the things that sat there so heavy on her tongue.

But the rain still drummed against the windows and the silence seemed sweet.

Instead, she fell asleep, curled up on Reza's chest with the fire dancing all over them both.

They came together in the night, too many times to count. She would roll, or he would shift, and it was as if the barest slide of skin against skin was too much. The first time they slid against each other he spread her out beneath him and kissed his way down her belly before settling between her legs and licking her into sobbing bliss. Another time she woke with his heat all along her back and his thigh thrust between hers. She couldn't help herself. She'd arched against all that hard, muscled heat until he'd shifted her, thrusting into her as he held her in place.

She lost track of how many times they woke and found each other in the dark. She couldn't count the number of times she fell apart, only for him to catch her there when they both fell back to earth.

The last time they woke together it was gray outside, with a hint of light across the sea. The rain had finally stopped. Reza lifted her over him and settled her on his lap, thrusting into her once again as he sat up, gathering her astride him.

It was her turn to set the pace and she took it slow, every last part of her body so tuned to him now it was as if they were one.

One body. One mind.

One heart, she thought, though she knew she shouldn't.

And the higher she climbed, the brighter that flame between them, the more she knew. What that raw thing was that took up more and more of her every time they touched. What was eating her alive from the inside out.

"One more time," Reza urged her as the sweet tension pulled tight, as she worked herself against him, hard and deep within her with his mouth against her neck. "Just one more."

And this time they broke apart together, soft and shattering.

She slumped in his lap, her forehead pressed to his, and tried to catch her breath while inside her everything was too raw. Too big, too unwieldy, *too much*.

Maggy might not have felt any of these things before. But it was like the salt in the air outside that had meant the sea was near. She knew what it was.

"Are you with me?" Reza asked, his voice low and gruff and, somehow, the sweetest thing she'd ever heard, as his hands moved gently up and down her spine as if he was bringing her back to earth with the slide of his hands over her skin.

Maggy couldn't move. She couldn't open her eyes. And she couldn't care less.

"I'm with you," she said, her mouth close to his, her head tipped into his. As close to him as it was possible to get. "I love you."

It took her another breath, long and still shuddery, to realize what she'd said.

And still one more to feel that Reza had turned to stone beneath her.

She pushed back so she could look at his face, and her heart broke. She felt it crack apart and splinter, there and then. Because he looked like a statue. Remote and inaccessible and more forbidding than she'd ever seen him before.

"Reza," she whispered. "Forget I said that. Let's just pretend—"

"No." He sounded something far darker than merely *rough* then. Much darker and much, much worse. He lifted her off of him, setting her to the side as if she was terribly fragile and required care, but then he moved out of reach. Fast. When his gaze met hers, Maggy saw nothing but blank, hard slate. "No. You cannot. That is impossible. And unacceptable besides."

CHAPTER NINE

"YOU DO NOT love me," Reza thundered at her, as if that could erase what she'd said. As if that could rewind this night. Shove it back in the bottle where he should have left it to begin with. "That is unacceptable on every level."

But there was an aching thing in his chest and he felt as if it might crack wide-open. And his body was as wrecked as if he'd gone out on a bender like a normal man might. Not that Reza needed drugs or alcohol when there was Maggy. She was infinitely more potent.

And he should never have let this happen. He knew exactly where it led. He'd been cleaning up the mess of it his whole adult life.

Maggy was still sitting in the middle of the vast bed where they'd hardly slept all night. Even now, he still wanted her. He stalked to his dressing room and threw on a pair of exercise trousers, letting them ride low on his hips. When he returned to the bedroom, she was standing by the side of the bed, buttoning herself into his shirt.

He didn't want to see how small and slender she was in his shirt. How long her legs were, naked and tempting, beneath the hem. When she was done buttoning it up, she lifted her chin and faced him, and he hated that she clearly needed to brace herself. Worse, she hugged herself around the middle as she studied him, too many things he didn't want to recognize clouding her pretty eyes and making him feel like the lowest bastard who had ever drawn breath.

Reza knew he was exactly that. But even so, he couldn't seem to ignore the part of him that urged him to go to her. To take her in his arms again. To make this right somehow, and no matter that she'd made a bad situation worse with the words she should never have said—but he couldn't do that.

"I didn't mean to say that," Maggy said, her voice quiet, though it seemed to punch into him all the same. "But that doesn't mean it isn't true."

"It cannot be true." He folded his arms over his chest and forced himself to stop admiring the way she looked in his damn shirt, as if he had as little control over himself as he'd exhibited this whole, long night. "This should never have happened." He jerked his chin at the bed between them. "Any of this."

He could see the instant she stopped feeling vulnerable—or decided to stop showing it, anyway. The exact moment that temper of hers kicked in. First there was that flash in her eyes. Then she frowned at him the way she hadn't done in some time, too busy smiling and folding her hands in her lap and learning how to exude good breeding with every breath.

"I have no idea what you're talking about." Her voice was even. Cool. "This is where all of this has been leading, surely. You didn't storm into my coffee shop in Vermont so we could end up polite and distant pen pals."

"I need a queen, not a lover," he threw her, and he did nothing to make the hit of that any less harsh than it sounded. Standing there at the foot of the bed where he'd shown her exactly the opposite all night long. He couldn't even tell who he was more furious with—her or himself. "I have no time to dally, and certainly not with you."

For a moment, he thought he might have broken her, and a sea of self-loathing washed over him, nearly taking him from his feet.

But this was his Maggy. His tough survivor. She'd made it through twenty years of dire circumstances. She'd sailed through the past weeks. What was an unpleasant conversation at dawn? He'd seen her mouth tremble, he was sure of it, but she only pressed her lips into a firm line and kept her chin high.

Reza had the dark, uneasy notion that he was the only one at risk of falling apart here. Something that seemed far more imminent when she moved toward him, skirting the bed and coming closer than she should.

Close enough that he could smell her again. Vanilla and coconut and, beneath that, her. His Maggy. He knew her now. Her scent, her taste. He'd had his mouth and his hands on every last inch of her body. His body stirred anew, which should have been impossible after the night they'd had. But nothing was impossible when it came to Maggy. Nothing at all.

He was in so much trouble. He was far past *trouble* and into a full-blown crisis.

"You're going to have to explain to me why the fact we had sex is a problem," she said, still in that quiet way of hers, suggesting she was under control. But he could see that sheen in her eyes, telling him otherwise. It made him feel worse. And more resolute at the same time. "Or why you freak out every time something happens between us. Shouldn't you want this?" She didn't wait for him to answer. "Why can't you have a queen *and* a lover?"

"This cannot happen," he bit out, his voice frigid, because the cold eating him from the inside out was the only thing he had. It was the only way he knew how to keep himself in one piece. "I am a king. I cannot allow anything to divert my attention from my responsibilities."

She shook her head, looking helpless for the first time in as long as he'd known her. "What are you talking about?"

"I have already told you." But it was harder now, wasn't it? He concentrated on keeping his hands to himself. And that scant bit of distance everything in him wanted to close. "I am a king. My focus must be on my people, not on the pleasures of the flesh. A king who loses his focus loses his way. Believe me."

"You're going to marry me." Her voice was fierce now, not cool at all, and there was a recalcitrant part of him that enjoyed that faint evidence that she was as shaken as he was. Reza didn't like to think what that made him. "You told me you want heirs. How did you think that would happen?"

"Not like this." He stepped back, putting distance between them the way he should have done from the start and keeping his damned hands to himself, no matter that he thought it might kill him. "I am a—"

"Stop saying that!"

He didn't know which one of them was more shocked when she shouted at him. She looked as surprised as he felt, though she couldn't have been. Reza wasn't certain anyone had ever raised a voice in his direction.

Why did it make him want to do nothing but gather her close to him again? What *was* this? Why was he still standing here, engaging in this conversation?

But he still couldn't move. He still couldn't leave her.

He was tearing himself apart.

"Stop it," she said again, her voice hoarse. "You're a king, yes. I know that. But you're also a man."

"That is the trouble," he grated out, unable to stop himself. Unable to keep himself in check the way he should. As if the tearing thing in him was a wrecking ball and he was splintering whether he liked it or not. "I must be more than a man. I must be above petty concerns. I am a creature of duty and honor, that is all. But you make me feel like a man and nothing more, Maggy, and I cannot have it."

Her face softened and that was worse. Much worse. "Reza—"

"Silence." His voice rang out, autocratic and regal. She stopped, making a faint sound, like a sob cut off before it could take root. But he was the king now. Not the man she could enchant and make into nothing more than her plaything. He had to be the goddamned king. "I should have delivered you to your brother the moment I found you. I should never have brought you here. I cannot allow *this* in my life."

"This?"

"You." He slashed a hand through the air. "I sit on a throne and hold the fate of a country in my hands. That must be my focus. That must be my *only* focus. My father split his focus and it cost him. He was blackmailed. Disgraced, if only privately. He nearly brought the country to its knees because he had a mistress he put before the crown. And his only excuse was *love*."

His voice was scathing, but she didn't back down. It was one more reason he couldn't have her. He couldn't risk it. "I don't know anything about your father, but you and I have been betrothed since I was born. You could have married someone else, but you didn't. Surely that means something."

"You died." His voice was so harsh. So cold. And he told himself he didn't care when she flinched. "And I moved on."

But Maggy had a spine of steel. She shook her head at him. "Clearly. That's what last night was about, I'm sure."

Reza ground his teeth together, and if his hands balled into fists and betrayed him, well. There was no way out of this. There was no fixing all the things he'd broken last night because he'd lost his hold on himself. There was only this, damage control and moving on.

He would not be his father, a disappointment to his wife, his son. A scandal on the throne, however hushed. A man who'd taken his own life and had left behind a son who had to clean up his mess. Reza had been twenty-four when he'd had to relocate his father's longtime mistress to one of the crown's far-off properties to keep her away from his mother and the royal court who'd despised her—and to keep her from blackmailing his father even after his death. He'd been paying for his father's mistakes—literally—ever since.

"I must marry and I must hold the throne," he told Maggy now, somehow keeping his voice in check. Somehow finding his control again. "These are the duties of every king of the Constantines across the ages. You make me imagine that I am something more than the throne. You make me feel as if I am a man instead."

"You *are* a man." Her voice caught. "You are the best man I know."

"I am a king," he gritted out, and if his chest felt crushed, too bad. He didn't want to be the best man she knew. He didn't *want* this. He couldn't want anything like it, because he knew where it led. To a small cottage on the Isle of Skye, where a wretched old woman lived with the memories of a man who had never been hers, a man she'd tortured into taking his life, and the kingdom she'd been willing to ransom to serve her own ends. To his father's early grave, the circumstances of his death hushed up and hidden, and a cloud forever over his name and legacy. "Do you know what happens when a king believes he is a man? When he acts like he is no different from the rest? He becomes it. He thinks with his sex, his temper. He allows himself to be flattered, to be small. To think in tiny terms that benefit him, not his country."

He saw her swallow, hard. "Those are all bad things," she said quietly. "But there are other ways to be a man. It's not all sex and temper and war and pain."

"I have spent my entire life keeping myself apart from the masses for the good of my kingdom," he told her, fierce and rough. "I will not throw away what I have built on a woman. I refuse."

"Reza." His name in her mouth was a revelation, still. And he hated himself for it. "Don't you think there's another reason you feel so out of control? Maybe you feel the same things I do. Maybe this is your chance to be a king *and* a man, not one or the other. Maybe you lo—"

"Never." His voice was too harsh then. It was beyond cold. It was nothing less than a slap—anything to keep her from saying that word. That impossible word. Love had no business here, with him. Love had nothing to do with the life he led, the kingdom he ruled. It had not one damned thing to do with that cracked feeling that was making his chest ache. "That will never happen. I will never allow it. *Never.*"

"Reza—"

But he couldn't allow her to stand there, naked beneath his shirt, all his temptations made flesh. It would be too easy to weaken, as he'd already proved. He had to end this. Now.

"I am summoning your brother," he told her, pulling the practicalities around him like a cloak. He moved around her, heading for the door, keeping his hands to himself no matter how little he wished to do so. "He will no doubt wish to carry you back to

Santa Domini like the lost treasure you are. I hope that when I see you again at some or other event, we can be cordial."

"Cordial? Are you out of your mind? Reza, we—"

He looked over his shoulder. "There is no 'we.' I release you from our contract."

She looked lost, but she still stood tall. And made him feel tiny in comparison.

"What if I don't release you?"

He shrugged as if he didn't care about this. About her. "Then you will feel very foolish, I imagine, when I marry someone else. Which I will, Maggy. And soon."

And then he walked out of that bedroom before he changed his mind the way he longed to do. Before he decided she was right and he could be both a king and the kind of man he'd imagined he was last night, sunk deep inside her. Before he went to her and kissed her mouth and took her back to his bed, the way every part of him shouted he should do, right now.

Before he let her make him forget who he was all over again.

Cairo Santa Domini was due to arrive on the island only a handful of hours later.

Maggy realized that Reza must have summoned him immediately after leaving her in his bedchamber. It suggested that the man must have leapt up from whatever kingly thing he'd been doing and raced to fly here, all to meet a sister he'd believed dead for twenty years.

"His Majesty expects the Santa Dominian plane to land in two hours," one of her smiling attendants told her when she'd made it back to her own room, still dressed in Reza's shirt. The idea of wearing the dress he'd taken off of her with such sweet skill made her want to die. She'd decided it was far better to give the staff a little show, in case they'd missed Reza carrying her through the halls last night—

But it was better not to think about last night.

"Thank you," she replied. Because what else could she say?

Maggy didn't know what to expect from a brother. Especially not when he was a famous man in his own right. Another king, no less. And she certainly didn't know how to feel. About anything, after a night that had scraped her raw and a morning that had left her feeling nothing but beaten up and bloodied.

She made her way to the state-of-the-art shower in her expansive bathroom suite and locked herself in. She made the water so hot the steam billowed up in clouds and first she scrubbed herself, over and over, trying to get him off of her. His scent, his touch. The memory of his mouth against her skin. Then she sank down, her back against the wall so she could tuck her knees up beneath her chin, and she cried.

For so long she thought she'd wrung herself dry, and yet she still didn't feel any better.

When she was dressed, in a shift dress over soft leather boots and a lovely cashmere wrap she would have called *princess casual* if anyone had asked, she stood for too long at her own mirror. Remembering when he'd stood behind her.

You need to stop, that caustic voice inside her, the one that had kept her safe all this time, snapped at her. *You're only making this worse.*

She went out into the villa while her attendants saw to her packing. Maggy expected Reza to ignore her. To stay out of her way. Surely that was the least he could do.

Maggy was picking at a meal she thought she should eat, though she wasn't the least bit hungry, when Reza strode into the breakfast room.

She gaped at him. She didn't pretend otherwise. She didn't try to hide it.

And she hated herself for the little sliver of hope that wormed its way into her heart—

But this was Reza. He said nothing. He didn't take back any of the things he'd said in his bedchamber. His gray gaze raked over her as if he was looking for evidence she was still her—but then he looked away again as he helped himself to some of the food the staff had set out on a side table.

He was hungry, apparently. He was the king— and that was all he wanted to be, the goddamned king—and he couldn't have someone fix him a tray. Of course not. Of course he had to come here and torment her.

"Are you trying to torture me?" she asked him, through gritted teeth.

There was no sign of the man she knew on his set face when he turned to her. No hint of silver in his faintly astonished gaze. It was as if the Reza she knew had been replaced by a stranger.

"I cannot imagine what you mean."

Maggy pushed to her feet. "If you want to do this, I can't stop you. Believe me, I spent my whole life with my face pressed up to some or other glass, wishing I could have whatever was on the other side. I'm not doing it with you."

That muscle clenched in his jaw, which she might have seen as a sign of hope twenty-four hours ago. But that was before that scene in his bedroom. That was before he'd thrown her out, like once again, she was nothing but garbage.

She'd thought becoming a princess would change that, but it didn't. Maybe it was something in her that made her so easy to dispose of. So easy to toss aside.

"No one asked you to," he said, and she told herself she was imagining the bite in his voice. As if this was hard for him when she knew it couldn't be. Because if it was, why was he doing it?

"I'm not going to stand here and let you talk to me like a robot." She threw her linen napkin on the table and pretended it was something harder and she was aiming for his face. "You might be one. You clearly *want* to be one. And you can hide all you want. But I won't take part in it."

And yet, after all her tough talk, she just stood there. She didn't *actually* beg him to reconsider. She didn't let him see her cry. But she might as well have.

He sat back in his chair, his mouth an unsmiling line that she wanted to taste. That was the trouble. She wanted him no matter what. No matter how little he wanted her.

"My investigators cannot be sure," he told her in his chilliest, most distant regal voice. "But they believe they've traced what happened to you."

Maggy wanted to hit him. And not with a linen napkin. But she wanted to hear this story, too. So she set her teeth and stood where she was.

"A man known to have been a member of the Santa Dominian military went on an unscheduled break not long after the car accident that killed your parents. Records trace him to London. Several weeks after that, a woman known to the British authorities after a botched drug smuggling attempt flew one-way to New York with a companion child. According to all records, the child named as that companion does not exist. The woman went underground soon after landing in New York City and was never heard from again. But three weeks later, you were discovered on that rural road in Vermont."

It shouldn't matter what the story was. She shouldn't care. "You think she was hired to throw me away across the Atlantic, far from anyone who was looking for me?"

She thought she saw a glimpse of the Reza she knew then—and it turned out, that was worse. The hint of compassion only made the cold that much more bitter when it claimed him all over again.

"I think if they wanted to throw you away, they would have left you in that car," he said softly. "I think someone took pity on an eight-year-old child. I suspect that woman was meant to care for you, not abandon you."

"Well." Maggy's voice was as cold as his. She could feel the chill of it. "That appears to be something I bring out in people. Over and over again."

Reza stared back at her and for a moment—only a moment—she was certain she could see something in his hard rain gaze. Something almost stricken. But it was gone in the next instant, leaving nothing but stone in its wake.

She told herself she was glad she felt empty inside as she walked from the room and left him there to his crown and his duty. Because the emptier she was inside, the less there was to hurt.

Maggy assured herself she was *relieved* when the Santa Dominian plane landed. During the ten minutes or so it took for the armored SUV to make it up from the airfield to the villa, she told herself what worked in her, leaving her feeling a little bit breathless, was happiness. Pure, unadulterated happiness. Because this was what she'd always wanted, wasn't it? A family. A home. And *without* having to make herself over into some Very Special Princess so she could marry a man she hardly knew.

You're just not used to all this happiness, she told herself stiffly. *That's why you feel like crying.*

Reza had never been anything but a diversion. He wasn't what she wanted. He'd been a means to an end, nothing more.

If she kept telling herself that, surely it would turn into truth.

And she was standing in the great open foyer when the SUV carrying Cairo Santa Domini pulled up in the circular drive, her hands in fists at her sides. Alone, of course.

Because she was always alone.

Buck up, Princess, she told herself. *You always will be.*

She heard a faint noise then and glanced over to find Reza beside her. He wore an expression she couldn't decipher on his face and his eyes were much too dark.

"You don't have to be here," she told him, because she couldn't stay quiet. That made her focus too much on all that emptiness. "I'm sure you have very important king things to do. Things that men would never do, only kings."

Reza let out a small sound that she thought was a sigh of exasperation. Maybe she only wanted it to be. Then, his mouth in that flat line that still seemed to kick up all that longing inside of her, he inclined his head in that way of his. And something was wrong with her that she felt that like some kind of support. As if he was holding her when he wasn't.

When he'd made it so clear he wouldn't.

Still, something inside of her curled at that. Like a small flame. Like hope that this thing between them wasn't finished. Not yet.

Maggy jerked her head away from him, focusing on what was happening outside in the drive. She watched as if she was far, far away as a man climbed from the back of the SUV without waiting for it to stop fully or for the hovering attendants to open his door. He stopped once he was out, and didn't move again until a redheaded woman followed him from the vehicle, then stood beside him, slipping her hand into his.

And there was no denying who he was. Cairo Santa Domini, known as an exiled king and a playboy of epic proportions before he'd taken back his kingdom. Maggy had stared at his face on tabloid magazines for years. It was hard to believe he was here. And more, that a vial of blood made them family.

Whatever that meant.

The woman—Queen Brittany, Maggy knew from the internet, once a reality star and a stripper and now the most beloved queen in Europe—gazed up at the man Maggy was supposed to call her brother as if she was giving him strength.

Cairo moved again then, his strides long as he headed for the villa's glass entryway, and Maggy couldn't breathe. Her palms stung and on some distant level she knew she was digging her nails into them, but she couldn't bring herself to stop. She could hardly manage to breathe.

Beside her, Reza shifted. Then, impossibly, she felt his hand in the small of her back.

She wanted to scream at him. She wanted to ask him what the hell he was doing. But she didn't want to do anything that would take the comfort of that hand away, no matter how cruel it was. No matter how little it actually meant.

Because that was the trouble. It was nothing to him. *She* was nothing to him, no matter how much hope she might carry deep inside her.

Yet to her, that hand was everything.

It was how she managed to stand there, straight and silent, as Cairo Santa Domini and his queen came swiftly into the hall. It was how she managed to breathe, just enough, as Cairo's gaze moved from Reza to her.

Then stuck on her.

He came closer and closer, every step loud against the marble floor, and then he stopped.

Dead.

Queen Brittany murmured something, but Maggy didn't hear it. It was only when Reza replied that she realized it must have been some kind of greeting. But Cairo was silent, too busy staring at her, and Maggy found she could do nothing but stare back.

Her heart was catapulting against her chest. Her ribs ached at the assault, or maybe because she kept holding her breath.

Because he had the same eyes. The same eyes she saw in the mirror every day. Caramel colored and shaped the same. *The same eyes.*

He muttered something in what she thought was Italian.

"There was a blood test," Maggy said, bracing herself to be thrown away the way she always was. "I'll do another one if you don't believe it."

She felt Reza's hand tighten at her back, as if he wasn't throwing her away after all. Or as if he didn't want to. Her nails dug deeper into her palms.

"You look like a ghost," Cairo said, his voice rough and reverent at once. "You look just like our mother."

Maggy's breath left her in a rush. "I'm not a ghost."

"No," Cairo agreed. He dropped his queen's hand and he moved closer, then stopped again. His gaze moved all over her as if he couldn't believe she was real. As if he wanted her to be real and was afraid she wasn't, after all. Or maybe that was her and her pounding heart. "You are Magdalena. You could not possibly be anyone else."

"Call me Maggy," she whispered.

And Cairo Santa Domini smiled, so bright it seemed to haul the sun inside, lighting up the foyer and Maggy's heart besides.

"Ah, *sorrelina*," he murmured. "I always did."

And then he closed the space between them and hauled her into his arms, lifting her off the ground and holding her close. Maggy was startled. He spun her around and she caught Reza's gaze over Cairo's shoulder. Silver and gray. It punched into her.

She sneaked her arms around Cairo's shoulders, her gaze locked to Reza's, to hug her brother back.

And she told herself she didn't care when the man she loved inclined his head again, then turned away.

She concentrated on the good things. The man who set her down on her feet and returned to studying her face, his gaze as over-bright as hers felt.

Just like a brother. *Her brother.* Just like a dream.

Except this time, it wasn't a dream. It wasn't a fairy tale.

This man was her family. Which meant, at last and for good, she belonged.

And that left room for that little flicker of hope inside of her to burn bright, then glow.

CHAPTER TEN

THE THRONE ROOM in Constantine Castle was used only for special occasions these days. Coronations, of course. Special ceremonies and addresses. Mostly, it was cordoned off and used as part of the tours that the public could take through some of the less private parts of the castle.

There was absolutely no reason that Reza should have found himself there, standing before the throne like some petitioner of old.

It had been weeks since Maggy had left the villa. Weeks since the world had learned that the Santa Domini princess had lived through that car accident twenty years ago.

She was now the foremost obsession of the international tabloids, just as Reza had predicted.

And it did not help that he knew exactly what it had taken for her to smile so graciously at the cameras. How hard she had worked to appear so elegant and so beautiful, every inch of her as beautiful as her mother before her and so startlingly, obviously a

Santa Domini that the fact it had taken twenty years to find her seemed like an outrage.

He told himself he only read these articles and watched the news reports to see how and when he was mentioned. But he wasn't. And Reza did not care to speculate as to why the Santa Dominian palace did not share the fact that he had been the one to find her.

The palace said very little, in fact. It had released a statement upon her return, announcing that she was recovered after all this time and enjoying getting to know her brother and the life she'd forgotten. Cairo had given an address that had expressed his joy at having some part of his murdered family returned to him. And the world had been forced to content itself with the very few pictures the palace released over those first few days. Maggy and Cairo together, laughing at something that made their identical eyes shine. Maggy holding the Crown Prince Rafael, her young nephew, while Queen Brittany looked on.

All very heartwarming.

Yet Reza remained cold straight through.

Here in this throne room, all the ghosts of his bloodline seemed to congregate. He could feel their disapproval press against him, like the weight of the formal crown he wore only on specific occasions these days.

He stared at the throne itself.

It was only a chair, though it dated back to the fifteen hundreds. It was made of finely polished wood and it gleamed in the sunlight that poured in through the stained-glass windows and made the room into a kind of chapel. A place of power and resolve, or so Reza had been taught.

He didn't understand the part of him that wanted to burn it. Rip it apart with his hands. Make it into so much kindling—

But there was no point in this kind of maudlin self-indulgence. He had let her go, the way he should have done from the start. From the moment he'd understood that he couldn't keep his distance with her. That she made him as bad as his father.

He had made his choice.

Reza made himself turn away. He pushed his way out of the great doors, nodding at the guards who waited there. He heard them muttering into their earpieces as they followed him down the grand hall. Alerting the rest of the palace to his movements. All hail his very public life that he'd lived blamelessly all this time. Forever apologizing for his father's failures. Forever making up for his father's sins.

For the first time in his life, Reza felt as if he was drowning. As if his role here was holding his head beneath the water. As if he had no choice but to open up his mouth, suck in the sea, and sink.

Impatient with himself, he shook it off as he rounded a corner and headed for his offices. Or he tried to shake it off.

Either way, he was as controlled and expressionless as always when he walked into his office to find three of his aides and his personal secretary waiting for him.

"Sire," his secretary said, and the man's deferential tone set his teeth on edge, when it was no different than it had ever been before. "There has been a development."

"You will have to be more specific," Reza clipped out as he rounded his desk, all of the historic city laid out before him on the other side of the windows. The far-off snowcapped mountains. The gleaming alpine lakes in the distance.

But all he saw was her face.

He gritted his teeth, then focused on his staff.

"The princess, sire," his secretary continued. Carefully. "She's given her first interview."

He did not play games and ask which princess his secretary meant, though there was a part of him—the cowardly part he would excise with his own fingers if he could—that wanted to hide from whatever this was a while longer. Even inside his own head.

"I imagine it will be the first of many," he replied. Reza felt more than saw the glances his staff exchanged, and braced himself. "I assume you are bringing this particular interview to my attention for a reason?"

His secretary stood straighter. "She discusses her wedding plans, sire. In some detail."

And it took every bit of Reza's training in diplomacy to simply stand there as if nothing was the matter. As if this news did not affect him in the slightest.

If only that were true.

"Have my felicitations sent with the appropriate gift," he murmured, as if he'd already forgotten what they were talking about. Then he treated them all to the full force of his stare. "Surely such things are usually done automatically, without my input?"

"I fear I cannot do the interview justice, sire," his secretary murmured. The man thrust a tablet onto the desktop and hit the play arrow on its screen.

Reza did not want to watch this. He wanted to hurl the tablet through the window behind him. He wanted to institute beheadings and reopen the old dungeons, and he wanted to start with the staff standing before him.

He wanted anything but Maggy in front of him, laughing with one of those American television journalists with alarmingly bright white teeth.

She was too beautiful. It was worse on-screen, where her marvelous cheekbones seemed more pronounced and her lively eyes seemed warmer and more kind than he remembered. Her voice was the same, soft and faintly rough, and all he could think about was Maggy on her knees before him, sucking him deep into her mouth.

Damn her.

He'd known she would be the ruin of him. What he hadn't realized was that even when he'd removed the temptation of her from his life, he would remain ruined.

"And I'm told you plan to honor the Santa Domini royal family's traditions, despite all these years away?" the interviewer asked.

"Oh, yes," Maggy answered, sounding as if the interviewer were her best friend in the world. Reza made a mental note to give his public relations team bonuses, given the magic they'd worked with her. She looked nothing like the mouthy shopgirl he'd met. She looked like who she was—who she had always been. Magdalena Santa Domini. "I have been betrothed to the king of the Constantines since I was born. And I am happy to honor my commitments. After all, not every girl gets to wake up one morning to find she's actually a princess and, even better, she's meant for a king."

The interviewer laughed but made one of those fake noises of concern that would have annoyed Reza had he been able to do anything but stand there, frozen, that aching thing in his chest threatening to break free at last.

"But you only just found out who you are," the interviewer said. "How can you rush into something like this?"

"The king is the one who found me," Maggy said, almost shyly, and Reza knew exactly why they'd held it back before now. For this moment. For maximum impact. He almost admired it—the Santa Dominis were nothing if not in complete control of their images. Why should Maggy be any different? "He knew who I was before I did. And we spent some time together as I adjusted to my new role." She smiled down at her lap, looking for all the world as if she was overcome with emotion. It set Reza's teeth on edge. Especially when she looked up again, now looking flushed. *Like a woman in love*, a voice inside him murmured. "I'm more than happy with my fate."

His hand shot out before he could control it, stopping the video. His heart kicked at him, making his ribs ache.

"If you continue, sire," his secretary said, even more carefully than before, "the princess claims the wedding will be in June."

"In June," Reza said. His voice sounded as if it was someone else's.

"Yes, sire."

"This June."

His secretary nodded.

Reza stared down at the tablet before him, frozen on Maggy.

He hardly knew himself any longer and it was her fault. He had spent his whole life keeping himself free of emotional entanglements, just as he'd been taught by both his mother's cold demands and his father's bad example. He was trying to rule a kingdom and Maggy was telling lies to the whole world, boxing him into corners he wouldn't be able

to get out of without causing an international inci-
dent and destroying the relationship between the
two kingdoms—

Reza paused then. He took a deep breath in, then
let it go.

She had thrown down a gauntlet. He would pick
it up.

Maggy might think she wanted the man. Reza
knew better. It was high time he showed her what
happened when she taunted both man *and* king.

"Have the helicopter ready in fifteen minutes."
His voice was smooth. Even. As if there was none
of that fire beneath it. As if he wasn't burning alive
where he stood. "I believe it's time I called upon my
lovely bride."

Maggy sensed him before she heard a sound.

She waited in one of the palace's grand salons,
set aside for visiting heads of state and various monarchs, sitting like the picture-perfect princess Reza
had made her. She'd been informed the moment his
helicopter had entered Santa Dominian airspace.
She'd been alerted when he'd landed.

But she didn't need anyone to come and whisper
in her ear that Reza was in the palace. That he was
being led straight to her. She could feel it deep in
her belly. She could feel it in the electric shivers that
traced patterns over her limbs and the butterflies that
performed calisthenics inside of her.

And then at last he was there, striding into the grand salon as if it was his, and it all got worse.

Or better, depending on how she looked at it.

Reza moved through her brother's palace the same way he'd strode into that long-ago coffee shop. He looked elemental. Regal stone and royal temper, all the way through.

She made herself stay where she was, and no matter that he bore down upon her like a freight train.

The doors closed behind him, leaving them alone in this overwrought room of antiques with priceless artifacts scattered about on every surface. But all Maggy could see was Reza.

"I knew you'd come," she said softly when he was in front of her, standing there radiating fury and something else she couldn't quite decipher in another perfectly pressed suit. "I'm surprised it took you as long as it did."

"You should have told me you were psychic," he replied, his voice all edges and threat. Yet it rolled through her like a caress. Like his body moving over her and in her—but she had to focus. "It might have saved me the time and the trouble."

Back in the villa, that might have killed her. But she'd spent a few weeks here, in the company of her marvelously wicked sister-in-law and her sharp, funny brother, and she wasn't the same person she'd been then. Or she was more that person than she'd known how to be that awful morning after.

And she'd seen through him, at last.

"You weren't discarding me, Reza," she told him softly, not beating around the bush because she'd already lost twenty years of her real life. She didn't want to lose a moment more. "I know you might have told yourself that you were. But what you were really doing was running scared."

As she'd known he would, he turned to granite.

"I beg your pardon."

She smiled at that, and it wasn't one of her fake, princess smiles. She felt this one down deep. "I love it when you say that, so stuffy and *indignant*. But it's true. I think you know it."

"The king of the Constantines does not *run scared*, I think you will find." Reza's brows arched, but he was still right there in front of her. He hadn't walked away again. "By definition."

"Perhaps not." She raised her own brows, settling back against the sofa as if, this time, she was the one gracing a high throne with her presence. "But what about you, Reza?"

"What about me?" He frowned at her. "I don't follow."

Of course he didn't.

"You have the king thing down, I think we can all agree." And he was so much the king. Even now, standing in another man's palace, he radiated that fierce authority. Maggy could feel it deep in her belly. "Are you really going to pretend that you're not also a flesh and blood man with his own needs?"

"I am not pretending anything. But I do not have to give in to my baser instincts. I do not have to let whatever needs I might have control me."

She thought he was speaking more to himself than to her.

"But you're okay with letting your dead parents and their terrible marriage control you instead." He looked outraged, but she'd expected that. She pushed on. "I did some research into your parents these last weeks. I dug up all those rumors. The speculation that your father was so wrapped up in that woman he nearly brought the country to war. That he disgraced the crown, then took his own life. All those nasty whispers."

"They are not whispers, they are facts I have kept from the public for years." He sounded starched through, though she could see that muscle in his cheek, telling her the truth about his feelings. "And now that you know these unsavory truths, there is no need for these theatrics, is there?"

Maggy folded her hands in her lap even tighter, because she wanted to reach for him.

"I didn't have any parents," she said softly. "But I'm pretty sure the point of them is that they're supposed to protect *you*, Reza. Not make you responsible for *their* problems."

"You have no idea what you are talking about." His voice was dark. Low.

Tortured.

"If you say so," she replied in a tone that told him she disagreed. Quietly. Then inclined her head the way he liked to do. "Your Majesty. You must know best."

And she thought for a moment that she could hear his teeth grit.

The truth was, she knew him. That had been the truth she'd returned to again and again in this time away from him, nursing that flame of hope deep inside of her. She knew him because she *was* him, in all the ways that mattered. He was as alone as she'd always been. He hid it in his palaces and villas, his bespoke suits, and his ranting on about what the king could and could not do—but he was always alone. His life was a throne, nothing more.

It might shine a lot brighter than her little room in Vermont, but it was the same narrow bed and the same cold thing inside that never quite warmed. Maggy knew this better than anyone.

She knew *Reza* better than anyone, in part because he'd shown her the pain behind his mask that dreadful morning.

He had found her and rescued her from a life that had never been meant to be hers. This was her chance to rescue him in turn.

"Exactly what is it you think you are doing?"

Reza asked her with soft menace, fierce danger all over his harsh face, but she couldn't allow herself to be intimidated. Not when it mattered this much. "Do you truly believe that you can announce a wedding date and I will simply honor it? Because you say so?"

"That was pretty much your original plan, if I remember it right." She shrugged. "Why shouldn't it work for me?"

"You should have told me you were barking mad," he gritted out. "I would have handled this whole thing differently."

"I'm not mad. I am mad *at* you," she retorted. She stood up then, letting her dress fall where it would. She'd chosen it carefully because it made her look like a queen and she knew it. She could see he knew it, too. "You made me into a princess. Now I want to be your queen. As promised."

His hands were clenched into fists at his sides. He looked like thunder. But he was here. He was *here*, and that was what kept her standing where she was, pretending her heart wasn't thumping and her stomach wasn't in knots.

"You cannot force me to marry you," he growled at her, as if that was the end of the matter. But he still didn't leave.

Maggy only smiled at him.

"First," she said, "it's not up to you whether you marry me or not. It's your destiny." She saw the moment he realized she was throwing his own words right back at him. It made those hard rain eyes go silver, and that was when she knew this would be okay. That it would work. That the flicker of light inside of her, hopeful and bright, had been guiding her in the right direction all along. "And second, you silly man, haven't you realized that we're made for each other? You took a scared, beaten-down woman and made her a princess."

"And you took a king and rendered him nothing but a man," he bit out, but she thought he sounded less furious than before.

She'd seen that gleam of silver and she wasn't afraid any longer. She'd already lost him, however briefly. She wasn't doing it again. Not ever again.

Maggy moved toward him, watching that muscle in his cheek flex as she did. She didn't stop when she drew near. She slid her hands up on his chest and she arched herself into him, never taking her eyes from his.

"I love you, Reza," she told him, from the very depths of her. "I love the king in you. I love how seriously you take your duties. I love how deeply it matters to you that you take care of your people. But it was the man who took care of me. And I love him more."

"Maggy…" he whispered, as if her name might break him in two. "I don't know how to do this. My father—"

"You are not your father," she told him, her gaze

solemn on his. "And I have no desire to be your mistress. And, Reza, no one knows how to do it. I think that's the point."

And she watched him break. She saw his eyes flash silver and bright. She watched the ice crack and all that heat pour out of him as his arms came around her, and then he hauled her even closer.

Bringing Maggy home at last.

"You knew I would come to you," he growled at her, his mouth so close to hers. "You knew I couldn't resist."

Her eyes felt much too full. "I hoped."

"And if I marry you, then what?" he demanded. "When you strip away my control and I am rendered nothing but a man lost without you, what then?"

"Then I will come and find you wherever you're lost," she whispered. "Just as you came and found me. And I promise you, Reza, I won't let you stumble. I won't make you a worse king. I'll try my best to make you a better man."

His hands seemed uncertain as they moved up to smooth her hair back from her face, and she felt her tears spilling over when he leaned in and pressed a soft kiss on her forehead.

"I think I've loved you all my life," he told her, his voice a rough sort of velvet she'd never heard from him before. It washed through her, heat and love. "I loved you in the abstract. I mourned you.

And then I saw you in that picture and I fell in love all over again."

He kissed her then, and it was a real kiss. Wild and dark and perfect, rolling through her and making her heart swell inside her chest. He kissed her again and again, as if they were making their vows here and now. As if they were fusing themselves into one.

When he pulled away again, it was her turn to reach up and cradle his face in her hands.

"When I was first found by the side of that road," she told him, "I dreamed of fairy tales. Kings and queens and palaces. Every night, for years, I would go to sleep and dream of fairy-tale stories filled with people I wanted so badly to believe were real." She smiled at him. She kissed him. "But maybe they were. Maybe they weren't dreams at all. Maybe they were the life I left behind me when that car crashed."

He whispered her name, drawing her closer.

"Reza." And her voice was a scrap of sound. "Don't you see? I've been dreaming of you my whole life. It's just that I forgot your name for a little while."

His smile then was the most beautiful thing she'd ever seen.

"I will endeavor to make certain you never do again."

"Marry me, Your Majesty," she whispered, tipping her head back and loving him with all she was, all she would be, all she'd ever dreamed she could be. Right here in his arms, at last. "Make me your queen."

That June, in a ceremony televised around the world and gushed over in all the tabloids, with her newfound family there to give her away and a brand-new country that had fallen in love with their king's lost princess, he did.

And they spent all their happily-ever-after together, making their fairy tale real.

Just as Maggy had always dreamed.

* * * * *

If you enjoyed this story, take a look at these other great reads by Caitlin Crews
THE GUARDIAN'S VIRGIN WARD
THE RETURN OF THE DI SIONE WIFE
EXPECTING A ROYAL SCANDAL
Available now!

And why not explore these other
WEDLOCKED! stories?
BOUND BY HIS DESERT DIAMOND
by Andie Brock
A DIAMOND FOR DEL RIO'S HOUSEKEEPER
by Susan Stephens
Available now!

COMING NEXT MONTH FROM

HARLEQUIN Presents®

Available February 21, 2017

#3505 SECRETS OF A BILLIONAIRE'S MISTRESS
One Night With Consequences
by Sharon Kendrick

Waitress Darcy Denton isn't Renzo Sabatini's type. But unworldly Darcy becomes addicted to their passionate nights. And then she discovers she's pregnant! Darcy dare not tell Renzo. But it's only a matter of months before he claims what's his...

#3506 CLAIMED FOR THE DE CARRILLO TWINS
Wedlocked!
by Abby Green

Cruz De Carrillo cannot forget kissing maid Trinity Adams. But Trinity quickly moved on—to become *stepmother* to his brother's sons! To protect his orphaned nephews and finish what he started, he'll have to put a ring on Trinity's finger...

#3507 THE INNOCENT'S SECRET BABY
Billionaires & One-Night Heirs
by Carol Marinelli

Raul Di Savo desires more than Lydia Hayward's body—his seduction will stop his rival buying her! Raul's expert touch awakens Lydia to irresistible pleasure, but his game of revenge forces her to leave...until an unexpected consequence binds them forever!

#3508 A DEBT PAID IN THE MARRIAGE BED
by Jennifer Hayward

Angelina's world is shattered when Lorenzo Ricci walks into her engagement party to tell her that she's still married to *him*! Lorenzo will use financial and sensual means to reclaim his wayward wife. Can they survive their tempestuous reunion unscathed?

HPCNM0217RA

#3509 PURSUED BY THE DESERT PRINCE
The Sauveterre Siblings
by Dani Collins

When Prince Kasim finds he's falsely accused Angelique Sauveterre of an affair with his future brother-in-law, he can't resist this feisty beauty himself! Angelique blossoms under Kasim's touch and surrenders. But can he give her more than passion and precious jewels?

#3510 THE TEMPORARY MRS. MARCHETTI
by Melanie Milburne

Cristiano Marchetti proposes to Alice Piper to fulfill the conditions of a will. But his real agenda is revenge—for leaving him years ago! That is until it seems the future Mrs. Marchetti might become more than Cristiano's *temporary* bride...

#3511 THE SICILIAN'S DEFIANT VIRGIN
by Susan Stephens

Luca Tebaldi is furious at Jennifer Sanderson for inheriting his brother's estate—he'll seduce the truth out of her! But this sensual innocent sets Luca's senses on fire, forcing him to confront what *she* is enticing out of *him*!

#3512 THE FORGOTTEN GALLO BRIDE
by Natalie Anderson

Zara Falconer's wedding to Tomas Gallo set her free, but an accident wiped Tomas's memory before he could annul their vows. When she discovers this tortured man is still her husband, she has to ask—will their passion bring back Tomas's memories?

Somehow Lydia was back against the wall with Raul's hands
on either side of her head.

She put her hands up to his chest and felt him solid
beneath her palms and she just felt him there a moment and
then looked up to his eyes.

His mouth moved in close and as it did she stared right
into his eyes.

She could feel heat hover between their mouths in a slow
tease before they first met.

Then they met.

And all that had been missing was suddenly there.

Yet the gentle pressure his mouth exerted, though blissful,
caused a flood of sensations until the gentleness of his kiss
was no longer enough.

A slight inhale, a hitch in her breath and her lips parted,
just a little, and he slipped his tongue in.

The moan she made went straight to his groin.

At first taste she was his and he knew it for her hands moved to the back of his head and he kissed her as hard as her fingers demanded.

More so even.

His tongue was wicked and her fingers tightened in his thick hair and she could feel the wall cold and hard against her shoulders.

It was the middle of Rome just after six and even down a side street there was no real hiding from the crowds.

Lydia didn't care.

He slid one arm around her waist to move her body away from the wall and closer into his, so that her head could fall backward.

If there was a bed, she would be on it.

If there was a room, they would close the door.

Yet there wasn't and so he halted them, but only their lips.

Their bodies were heated and close and he looked her right in the eye. His mouth was wet from hers and his hair a little messed from her fingers.

"What do you want to do?" Raul asked while knowing it was a no-brainer, and he went for her neck.

She had never thought that a kiss beneath her ear could make it so impossible to breathe let alone think.

"What do you want to do?" He whispered to her skin and blew on her neck, damp from his kisses, and then he raised his head and met her eye. "Tonight I can give you anything you want."

Don't miss
THE INNOCENT'S SECRET BABY,
available March 2017 wherever
Harlequin Presents® books and ebooks are sold.

www.Harlequin.com

HARLEQUIN

Presents®

We can't wait for you to read *Secrets of a Billionaire's Mistress* by Sharon Kendrick—a tale of inescapable passion! Darcy and Renzo are about to experience a romance like no other...

Waitress...

Neither tall, willowy nor sophisticated, waitress Darcy Denton knows she isn't Renzo Sabatini's usual type. But, enthralled by the powerful magnate, unworldly Darcy becomes addicted to their passionate nights together.

Mistress...

Ensconced in Renzo's secluded Tuscan villa, Darcy glimpses Renzo's troubled past and desolate soul. She knows she should end it before she gets in too deep—but then she discovers she's pregnant!

Wife?

Harboring her own childhood secrets, Darcy dare not tell Renzo. But as the mother of his child it's only a matter of time—nine months, to be exact—before he claims what's his...

Don't miss

SECRETS OF A BILLIONAIRE'S MISTRESS

Available March 2017

Stay Connected:

www.Harlequin.com

f /HarlequinBooks

🐦 @HarlequinBooks

📌 /HarlequinBooks

HP06045